Midrash on the Juanitos

S0-ADD-755

Russell Rathbun

Midrash on
the Juanitos

didactic novella

Russell Rathbun
Cathedral Hill Press, St. Paul, MN

Art by Jim Larson

Copyright 2010 Russell Rathbun

Cathedral Hill Press, 1043 Grand Ave #213, St. Paul MN, 55105

Printed in the United States on acid-free paper

Library of Congress Cataloging-in-Publication Data
Rathbun, Russell.
Midrash on the Juanitos : a didactic novella / Russell Rathbun ;
art by Jim Larson.
    p. cm.
ISBN 978-0-9742986-4-1 (pbk. : alk. paper)
1. Christianity—Fiction. 2. Las Vegas (Nev.)—Fiction. I. Title.

PS3618.A856M53 2010
813'.6—dc22

                                    2010008735

ISBN 978-0-9742986-4-1

Contents

Chapter 1

We were somewhere in a third ring exurb perched on
the edge of our barstools when the drugs took hold. I
remember saying something like, "Maybe that wasn't
such a good idea. I think you should take me home." I
turned my head to tell him again, and as I turned the
whole bar came with me. When my head stopped at
nine o'clock, the bar came to a graceful halt and then
pulled itself back into place by some kind of slow-
acting, giant rubber-band mechanism.

I sat there staring at the side of my attorney's face,
feeling the not unpleasant undulations of the floor,
my stool making its way up one side of the swells and
picking up a little speed on the way down. He was
talking to the bartender, a fourteen-year-old kid with
a sandblasted face and pimento-stuffed green olive
eyes who thought he worked in the city, instead of this
pseudo-Irish O'pub on the manufactured Main Street
of the developer-planned old downtown of Maple
Lakes, established 2003. He was wiping the bar with

an eager casualness, acutely aware of himself as a real bartender, having a real bartender conversation with a real bar customer. I could see in his clench-jawed smile that he thought the act required more than he was bringing to it.

Idiot John, my attorney and confessor, had no such self-consciousness about him, his gelatinous jowls flopping out of time with the endless opening and closing of his mouth as he talked.

My attorney had come out from the city to check up on me; he said he was worried about me. I had not talked to him much since my troubles. Some people called it "my time away." My freak out, the fire, the revelation and de-revelation. I never knew what to call it. But I was doing pretty well, and part of my self-imposed treatment plan was to avoid my attorney.

Idiot John is my closest confidant, but he fails to encourage healthy thinking and mental wellness. He is a great encourager of my predilection for conspiracy and revolutionary world-saving, unmasking, anti-Christ-exposing, dark abyss falling into-ness.

He is a six foot four, two hundred and ninety pound Norwegian Irish Catholic Biblical literalist who doesn't believe in God. To allow the existence of the deity, he says, would affect the objectivity of his investigations. He is a tax attorney with the largest firm in the state, and from everything he tells me,

he is very good at his job. Which I believe because he is very good at everything he does. He is voraciously good at everything he does. Unfortunately one of the things he does is to get me to go to bars in the middle of the day and pull the ripcord on a mind that has been carefully coaxed into ignoring the voices of alarmist dissatisfaction with current cultural realities.

I had mostly been ignoring his phone calls, and making excuses when I answered. When he showed up at the church today, I thought it was best to get him out of there as soon as possible. It is not that he is disturbing or disruptive to the other pastors and associates—they all love him, and incomprehensibly he knows the name of everyone he talks to, from the people in reception to the administrative photocopy appointment people to the senior pastor. I have a hard time recognizing most of them.

It is his affect on me that I worry most about.

Anxiety is a lurky, insidious disorder that feeds not only on truly anxiety-provoking situations but memories of associations with anxiety-provoking situations or possibilities of memories of associations with anxiety-provoking situations. My attorney, for a myriad of reasons, gets the anxiety demon burning in my bones, and I fear a full-scale panic attack in front of my colleagues, whom I have spent the last six months trying to convince I am better.

To get him out of the church, because the devil was moving its way from my bones into the muscle layer and threatening to erupt through my skin and climb up and clamp that tight metal band around my skull, I agreed to have lunch with him. Then I agreed to sit at the bar and have lunch with him. Then I agreed with him that it was too late to turn back and I gave in.

Content to think and stare at Idiot John's mouth opening and closing, pretending that he was speaking my thoughts, trying to make the words in my head correspond with the pauses and rhythm of his jawing, I try to retrace the steps of my undoing. Step One:

Riding over here in his fourteen-year-old Toyota Celica, winding our way though parking lot after parking lot, my attorney looked at me and placed his voluptuous hand palm flat against my sternum, sending his Chi directly into my core. He said, "You don't seem O.K. You seem anxious." Which is guaranteed to give the demon a boost.

"No," I tell him. "I'm fine. I'm good. I have been doing really well."

"You are not, you have not been. Look at you. I can tell. You're a mess. Is this what you have been like? Every time you told me things were *good*? I knew it; see I knew it. That is why I came out here. Pretending you don't think what you think doesn't mean it's gone. Everything is waiting in there." He pressed harder on my chest and took his hand away. "As your attorney I advise you to let it out." I felt something drop on to the back of my neck, fingers spidering their way around my throat and up the base of my skull. He saw me trying to maintain. "Reverend, Reverend! It's hard to see you this way. I thought your doctor prescribed something for you."

"He did," was all I could manage. I had Ativan and Lunestra from my primary physician. I had Xanax from the psychiatrist, Vicodin and Valium from my mom and sister respectively. It is amazing how easy it is to amass a substantial drug collection almost by accident. "Take something then. As your attorney I demand that you take something."

"Okay, at lunch."

At the bar he got into my book bag, found my stash, and started sorting through the prescription bottles. He selected a few pills and went into his pocket for one more. He ordered two beers and put three pills in my hand. He told me to close my eyes and take the meds followed by four long swallows of the pale ale and in seconds I would be feeling a profound sense of well-being.

Why did I do it? This is the problem with my attorney. I always do what he tells me to do. In the moment I believe him. And I desperately wanted a profound sense of well-being. I could do a very simple thing like close my eyes and swallow pills with beer for a profound sense of well-being.

I finished the beer and had moved on to a Bloody Mary as the profundity began seeping into my synapses, firing slowly but indeed profoundly. The swells began to subside, and my stool righted itself on the fake wood floorboards. Idiot John's words were becoming audible. He was saying something about the antichrist. I thought, that seems interesting. The olive-eyed boy made a final pass with the bar towel and went to help someone else. I smiled, my head still locked at nine o'clock. Idiot John looked me up and down. "You seem better," he said.

That was Step One in the undoing. Step Two necessarily proceeds from Step One, because had I not been riding the profound sense of well-being, I would never have had the following conversation. Because … well … because until my attorney showed up I had been trying to be normal.

I had an experience some time ago in which I convinced myself that the church I worked for was part of a massive conspiracy to quietly control the world through a seditious mixture of Capitalism and false doctrine and that perhaps the world might have already come to an end. Ideas—all of which were encouraged, if not created, by my attorney. This led to the destruction of personal property—mostly my own personal property—and a brief hospitalization. So when it came to biblical concepts, I tried to focus on … . well, stuff having to do with being a good person and encouraging individual prayer life and understanding the awesomeness of god in worship. Not really biblical concepts, in other words.

My therapist had recommended that I not read the Bible at all, noting that it seemed to agitate me. But being a preacher, that would have been difficult. So I agreed to read as little as possible for my sermons and not think about what I was reading too much.

"What were you telling that kid?" I asked my attorney, indicating the bartender with my head.

"Who, Brian?"

"Yeah, the bartender kid."

"Brian. His Mom wants him to go to some tiny repressed Bible college so he doesn't get led astray by, you know, working at T.J. O'Tooles or whatever this place is."

"But what about the antichrist?"

"You know, one thing leads to another, I forget how we got onto it. Temptation, maybe. I told him not to worry too much. The antichrist is dead."

"The antichrist is dead?

"Oh, yeah. Dead. He died probably, I don't know, eighteen hundred years ago."

See, this is how Idiot John gets me into trouble.

He says stuff and I believe it. Not the slightest notion of doubt. He doesn't make suppositions; he makes declarations. And his declarations are what get me in trouble. My therapist is a little bit right. Reading the bible does agitate me, but it doesn't agitate me. It is the world that agitates me. I am fine when I don't read the bible or think about what I read in the bible because I can look at everyone else and smile and act like they act and shop and download and stream and derive nearly authentic pleasure from life. But when I read the bible and then look at the world—the disconnect I see between the possibility, authenticity, heartbreak-beauty of living a walking-in-love life and the living a watching-a-flat-screen life of pleasant regard—well that is when the dark abyss opens up and I feel it drawing me in. The compulsion to throw myself in becomes almost overpowering, and the only hope I have is to try to heave myself across to the other side. The attempt to do so usually looks like a spiral of obsessive and paranoid behavior. If I can feel and hurt and long and love—and get other people to feel and hurt and long and love—it is like throwing a plank across the abyss. Every person I reach is another plank. We can cover that damn thing up. But—and this is where the paranoia comes in—it really does start to look like there are forces at work that are trying to pull those planks up and return people to shopping-downloading-flat-screen-living pleasantness.

But, that is not real, my therapist assures me. The abyss has nothing to do with truth or lack of truth. It is simply a chemical imbalance in my brain and, as a result, I attach these feelings to the bible or to my workplace. For some people, their feelings draw them toward a popular musical personality or a political figure. So I need to avoid "triggers" and focus on making a healthy and productive life in the world I actually live in. These are the things my therapist tells me, and I have been fairly successful. I have maintained equilibrium. Maintained equilibrium by avoiding "triggers."

Triggers? My attorney, it has now occurred to me, drove out from the city with a loaded gun for the sole purpose of handing it to me. He does not agree with my therapist and the chemical imbalance theory. He believes in the world imbalance theory, and I know now that he is on a mission. This realization does not alarm me because of my profound sense of well-being; this no doubt was part of his plan. This, it also occurs to me, might be a downside of the drug induced profound sense of well-being. It doesn't seem to correspond to actual events in the world. I should, at this point, be alarmed. My mental health, my job, my ability to live a stable life are at stake.

How did it not register earlier when he pulled that gigantic gun out of his shoulder holster and laid it on the bar? Antichrist! He manipulated that entire conversation with young Brian O'Toole, whose mother is right—it isn't good for him to work in a place like this. Antichrist! But I do not run. I am very happy and I feel beautifully intrigued by my attorney's machinations.

I picked the gun up off the bar and cocked it.

"How do you know that the antichrist died eighteen hundred years ago?"

"How do I know?" He looked at me like I'd asked him how he knew what time it was. "It's in the bible."

I pulled the trigger. I was triggered. Any hopes that I would stay away from this thing—shot. "It's in the Bible?"

"It's in the Bible, Reverend."

"Really, because I have read the Bible a lot and I don't ever remember reading that." I am feeling good and not remotely in danger. Unaware that the world has just lost its balance, that the bar is tilting radically, and that stools and tables and drinks are skittering down the incline, I am enjoying myself and I want to encourage more declarations.

"Well," he says. "It doesn't actually report his death, but you have to figure he was probably pretty old when it was written, and that was around one hundred CE, give or take twenty years on either side. So, even if he'd lived to be a hundred or a hundred and fifty he never saw the third century."

"Who is he? When what was written?"

"Reverend, I am surprised at you. And you say you read your bible." He is so good at this. Knows exactly how to bring me along. "Well there is only one place in the holy book where The Anti gets a mention. You should know that Reverend."

I am thinking, I should know that. "Only one place?"

"Only one place—the Juanitos."

"What?"

"The Little Johns."

"The Little Johns?"

"The First, Second, and Third Epistles of John."

"The Juanitos."

"The Anti appears but five times in the good book, four times in the first letter of John and once in the second letter of John. And every single time it is used, who is it referring to Reverend?"

"Caesar? Rome?"

"Guess again."

"Um, the Jewish leaders?"

"Wrong 'em boyo."

"I don't know." He is drawing things out. He knows he's got me.

"A fellow leader in the beloved community of John—the church in Ephesus. Not the empire, not the dark powers of the demonic, but he lets fly on a brother. A church squabble, and from that minor usage a legend was born."

Oooh, the Juanitos. How I instantly and completely love the Juanitos. My attorney is a beautiful man—*everything I need, he gives it to me-e-e—everything I need he gives it but not for free*—it's hateful, and I'm so grateful.

"The Juanitos. You should really take a read. Truly some unlikely books for sanctification. Juan Uno is fine—edifying I would say. Juan Dos: Just a summary of the first one. Just grabs the key sentences, fifteen verses. I say leave in the original, we don't need to see the Cliff's Notes right after. And Senior Tres Juanito? Have you read it?"

I thought I had read it. I mean, I probably had read them like one time before, but that would have been in one of those "committing myself to read the whole Bible or read the Bible in a year" phases, which I have to admit I never really followed through on. So maybe I never really had read them before.

"I can't remember."

"Well of course you can't. There is nothing there."

"What do you mean?"

"I mean in that half a page that comprises the whole of the book of Three John, the shortest book in God's word, there is not one mention of Jesus, not one iota of doctrine, no Didicae—no nothing."

"Come on."

"If you can tell me, Good Rev. Lamblove, why that book is in the Bible I will be eternally grateful."

That was Step Two. My recovery was lost. My mind unwound. I had fallen. And I don't know if it was the mixture of prescription drugs and alcohol, but I became unraveled. I fell apart into freedom.

"I want to go." I told my attorney.

"Sure," he said. "I should get back too."

He pulled through the circular drive and dropped me at the office entrance of the church. I pulled up on the handle of the car door, maybe a little too hard, and it slipped out of my hand and snapped back down.

"Hold on there," Idiot John said. "It's locked. Let me come to a complete stop first. What's the hurry? You're not gonna run off and start reading the Bible right away, are you?"

I looked at him sharply, trying to show reprimand at his teasing and denial of his accusation, coming off, I am sure, a little crazed. He hit the electric lock, I grabbed my bag, the gun inside knocked against the car as I jumped out slamming the door on his self-satisfied laughing. How did I let him do this to me? I was in trouble.

Chapter 2

I need more light. Maybe a brighter bulb in the overhead. It has one of those industrial cage things around it, though I am sure it comes off easily with a screwdriver or something. I take out the Mead three-hole college ruled spiral I stole from one of the adult Sunday school classrooms and add screwdriver to the list. Then I remember to add: *Lamps (?), possibly brighter light bulb (full spectrum?).* This room is windowless and in the subbasement a little full spectrum might keep things from slipping.

This is a remarkably big place—for a closet. Probably ten feet by six feet. I could easily put a cot in here. I make a note in the Mead: *camping cot from...?* The pipes that run across the ceiling make the room sauna-ish, which I like. Sweating out the poisons, toxins, and confusion. The ceiling must be ten or twelve feet high. Headroom. I need the headroom for my project.

There's a mop bucket/sink kind of thing, consisting of an eight-inch tall concrete square sitting on the floor with a drain in the middle. The faucet is about three feet off the ground with a short hose attached. I could bathe in it. If it comes to that, I mean, that kind of time. I feel it is best to prepare for how ever long it takes. It could be a day or weeks. Something about weeks makes the top of my head glow.

After Idiot John dropped me off I went scouting for a place to use as a base while I worked on the new project. I didn't go to my office first to drop my coat and bag. My office is not safe. It is filled with gelatin. I move in slow motion in there. My mind slugs barely fast enough to keep the engine running. Here I am moving faster than I have for so long. Things were just going and moving and coming back, instances, urges, prodings refocusing and dropping into prepared slots in my head, the flywheel coming up to speed. Whatever it was I had done to get healthy was draining out the bottoms of my feet as I walked the halls and descended the staircases. Maybe not draining out—being pushed, slowly forced out of my feet by the hypodermic plunger my attorney had fitted onto my head. My mind was filling up with possibilities and a kind of electricity that put a steady fluid pressure on the health I had acquired.

I looked through the unused classrooms and the office in the old library to find a place, but nothing seemed remote enough. I had things to do that required me to be free to… well free of whatever being around people that were politely concerned for me and pleased by my efforts at recovery would bring me. I needed a place that had nothing in common with the sheen of faux wood office furniture with a built-in keyboard tray that slides under the desk for all the times when you pretend you don't spend most of you time in the office humping your computer. This was my Sun Dance and I didn't want the federal government coming in and telling me what I could and couldn't do.

The Native American tribes who practiced sun dance were: The Arapaho, Arikara, Asbinboine, Cheyenne, Crow, Gros, Ventre, Hidutsa, Sioux, Plains Cree, Plains Ojibway, Sarasi, Omaha, Ponca, Ute, Shoshone, Kiowa, and Blackfoot tribes.

Of all the cards and wishes of wellness I received in my brief (comparably brief—compared to the human gestation period, say) hospitalization, the only sentiment or gesture or expression that did not fill me with shame, tortured embarrassment, and not a little self-loathing turned back on the instigator, was an article torn from a *National Geographic Magazine* that appeared to be decades old. It was folded roughly to fit in a Hallmark size envelope. Next to the article's title—*The Sun Dance of the North American Tribes*—

my well-wisher had drawn a small smiley face with a blue ballpoint pen. The line that formed the smile was asymentrical, almost a smirk. A lovely smirk that I was sure that I knew. Her sentiment, for whatever reason, made me feel like the world was not plastic, flat-packed, thin and simple, all of which made me smile. I read the article over and over, several times a day when confronted with group therapy—"*Confronting denial through the arts*" or "*Understanding your medications.*" The article was deep and calming breaths. I would recite passages randomly to reassure myself or they would impose themselves on my mind.

When I pushed through the fire door and found these steps to the sub-basement my feet grew dry and tingly. This was the right direction. At the bottom of the stairs I looked around and saw all the furnace and boiler stuff, the water meter, gas meter, telephone demarcation box, circuit panels, a door at one end of the room marked "storage", and next to it a door marked "utility closet". I didn't even open the "storage" door. "Utility" was what I needed. Storage is where I had been. Up above ground in my office every day, working my treatment plan, writing down pleasant thoughts, saying them in a pleasant voice. The prospect of asking real questions, doing real work, reading and not knowing, *actually* caring, "*If you can tell me, good Rev. Lamblove, why that book is in the Bible I will be eternally grateful.*" Oh, am sure you will Big Juan, I am sure you will. Utility, to again be useful, to provide some thing of utility to the greater community, this is where I will be working. Working on the Bible like a line man or a sewer worker—going down, dropping through the street, under the city. Deep work—I should get a hard hat.

The door to the Utility closet was unlocked, and though I had a master key I didn't go in. I opened the door halfway, saw a workbench and shelves full of old cleaning supplies and my mind made a sort of "fwoong, click" sound. I walked, I'll say rapidly, back up the two flights of stairs and through the halls to my office to wait for everyone to go home before I moved in, some last appearance of cooperation with the powers. I am not yet outright rejecting the pills nurse—plastered, patient smile—hands me; just tucking them into the back of my cheek until she leaves and I can spit them out.

I went into my office, shut the door quietly and turned off the light. I sat down behind the desk. I got up from behind the desk and turned on the light. I opened the door slowly, slightly, checked the hall and pulled back in—this time locking it. I turned off the light, went back to my desk and sat down. I was surprised to find most of the gelatin had melted and I could move around more easily, almost at the speed

I desired, my thinking unstilted, lean, without slug.

I realized I still had my book bag hanging across my body from left shoulder to right hip, something hard and unfamiliar digging in when I moved. I stood up and pulled the bag over my head and set it gently on the floor. Then, thinking it was hot—though I could feel the institutional reconstituted Frigidaire on the back of my neck—I took off my suit coat and shirt. Standing there in my V-neck, nipples getting hard, I realized that I must just be preparing for it to get hot. Perhaps I thought, soon I would be hot, knew by intuition it would be hot, but certainly was not yet hot. I threw my coat and shirt on the floor and sat back down, pulled the Readers Gift Bible on the desk over in front of me. It was an extra from last Sunday's Pastor's Class for Young People Graduation—the feeble adulthood ritual. I pulled it out of its cellophaned, cardboard gift box and broke the seal. I inhaled deeply, shuddered and coughed.

I turned on the desk lamp, wiped my mouth with the back of my hand and thumbed my way to the Juanitios and read. I read One; I read Two; I read Three and then turned back to the beginning and read them all again. I had the time. The best way to begin this project was to ingest the material. Ingest as much as possible and let it start to work. I had another round. I was starting to feel it. The first round through started to relax me. The second round made me sleepy. The third round I could start to feel the jockey urging me on, giving me my head. My Attorney was right about this stuff. There are crazy questions and contradictions, cliffs and ravines everywhere. I was reading to fall. And then in the grips of the cavalier excitement that was overtaking me it occurred to me to read them in reverse order to try and flush out something to wrestle with.

The Sun Dance is a ceremony practiced differently by several North American Indian Nations, but many of the ceremonies have features in common, including dancing, singing and drumming, the experience of visions, fasting, and, in some cases, self-torture.

First I stripped out the Characters.

Taking them in reverse order I can get a frame or a grip, reverse engineering—I can identify the characters and tease out what's at stake.

Tres Juanito, unlike Uno, is an actual letter. It begins:

The Elder to the Beloved Gaius, whom I love.

Here we have the addresser and the addressee. The Elder, the author, is presumably also the author of Dos and presumably the author of Uno, although that seems not as likely given its clear group authorship by the use of the We continually. The Elder is probably not John the disciple John. The notes in the Readers Gift Bible say it was written around 100 CE. If that's correct—and why wouldn't it be?—then the letters identified with John almost certainly come out of the Christian community that John established, probably around Ephesus.

Even with the flush of the Readers Gift Bible working on me, I think of that blue ball-point smiley face. Did she run across the article and think I would find it interesting, adding the smiley face in lieu of a signature or a note, understanding that nothing like, *I hope you are well* or *Get well* or *I am praying for you* would express anything like what the words attempted to signify? Did she remember it from a previous reading and seek it out—intending it as a comment (or guide?) to what she thought I might undergo? Or perhaps knowing, *knowing* there would be a time like this when I would need to act to undo all my healing.

In Greek "the elder" can be someone who holds a significant position in the community or simply an old man. He must have had some position of authority—I mean they put some of his books in the Bible—but I really pick up an old man vibe from him. And as for authority it seems from the letters that he is kind of losing his authority, or it is being challenged, or more likely he has lost what ever fight these letters refer to,

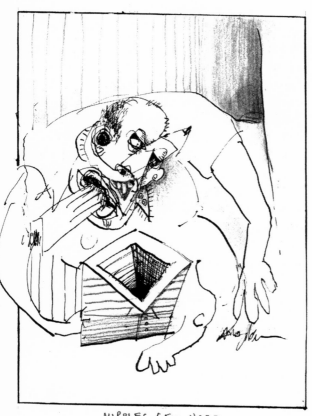

NIPPLES GET HARD

although he is not quite ready to admit it. He seems tired and scared and angry. Bitter even—a little bitter.

He writes a fairly standard form of the Greek letter: the opening address, the praising of the recipient. *Dear Gaius.* Although the praise is standard to the form, methinks he doth praise too much. The Old Man identifies Gaius as one of his children, that is, on his side of the fight, but his over-the-top ingratiating seems to suggest some doubt on the Old Man's part. Gaius is obviously in a different location than the Old Man, and he seems to be at the heart of the action. The Old Man writes how recent "friends who have arrived" told him how hospitable Gaius was when they visited wherever it is that Gaius is and the Old Man is not. It also seems to be the location of the church the Old Man mentions several times. The Old Man is in exile from the church—maybe the church at Ephesus. Which would make sense since many people believe that Paul had a connection to the Community established by John.

The Church where he is writing to Gaius, is also the location of his adversary, Diotrophes. Diotrophes is in power, possibly having usurped the Old Man. In the letter he complains, "I have written something to the church; but Diotrophes, who likes to put himself first, does not acknowledge our authority. So if I come, I will call attention to what he is doing in spreading false charges against us. And not content with those charges he refuses to welcome the friends, and even prevents those who want to do so and expels them from the church." (3 John 9-10)

So it's an ugly situation. The Old Man believes that a heretic has taken over a church that he'd started and mentored. This heretic, Diotrophes, seems to be spreading false charges against the Old Man, maybe making claims of false teaching as a way to throw him from power. As a result it appears that the Old Man was exiled from the church (taking a remnant with him) or is simply an itinerant after the model of Jesus's disciples—starting churches, revisiting them on a circuit, and sending letters to instruct them in his absence. Whatever the situation it is clear the Old Man, once maybe truly seen as The Elder, is not welcome. Neither are those who side with him. He says in his letter that even those who want to "welcome the friends" (meaningthose sympathetic to him) are prevented and expelled from the church.

Now, it's curious that Gaius is praised for welcoming the friends, yet there seems to be no issue of him being expelled from the church. Which means either the "friends" to whom Gaius showed hospitality were not seen as siding with the Old Man, or it is clear to Diotrophes that Gaius' loyalties lay with him and not the Old Man. This is what the Old Man wants to find out. This is purpose of the letter. He is sending Demetrius—who he trusts—to Gaius to check out the situation. *I am sending you to Gaius to see where his loyalties lie. Is he still a friend of the truth or has he gone over to the dark Diotrophes and the father of lies. Take this letter and see how he responds. Now away with you—be quick.* That kind of thing. He sends Demetrius to test the hospitality he so praised, and he makes it clear that to refuse to welcome Demetrius is to "imitate what is evil" (namely Diotrophes).

The Old Man, Diotrophes, Gaius, Demetrius. I scan my bookshelves and pull down anything that might relate, enlighten.

The Old Man, Diotrophes, Gaius, Demetrius. I read. I scan and skim, look up and cross-reference.

The Old Man, Diotrophes, Gaius, Demetrius.

I look around for something to write on. There are pink While-You-Were-Out phone message things and the back sides are blank but too small. I thumb the Readers Gift Bible to the back, past the maps to the appendices and stop on one titled, *Having a Fruitful Alone Time* and uncap a Uni-ball Vision Elite Bold .005 and begin to write over the text. First impressions third time through the Juanitos:

Description of Characters, compiled from *The Johannine Epistles*, Bultman; *A Love Supreme*, Callahan, Alworth's *Encyclopedia of Legends from the Early Church*, notes from the Readers Gift Bible, Spire Publishers, Cincinnati, OH, *Amazing Martyrs and Their Friends*, Friar Tuck Press (comic book) and wild-but-almost-instinctual-speculation.

The Old Man: He is the heir to the leadership of the beloved community, the one literally following in apostle John's footsteps. Scholars have some notion (or maybe not really scholars, but I have some notion somewhere in my head from all these books) that Jesus didn't walk around all the time just because he had to get somewhere and walking was the only way to do it, but that he was embodying what he was saying. Jesus was not teaching a stay-in-one-place, come-to-an-end, answer-located-here, kind of a truth. And his disciples, if they did not get a lot of things, seemed to get that. They walked around, they spread. And you don't walk alone. Find friends, teach them, take them with you, take them on the way, walk and talk. They went to towns and they taught. Walk, their teacher taught them, and they did. Those that heard and believed gathered together, met, prayed, talked, tried to live by this other way—churches, these gatherings came to be called. So these walking, itinerant, move-about disciples would come back around to these towns and check on how the people in the churches were doing, give them the news from other churches, teach more, repeat the stories the teacher had told them. The Old Man was once removed from those first itinerant teachers. The apostle John was his mentor/teacher/rabbi, and John had walked with Jesus, and the Old Man had walked with John. It seems that John's home base was in Ephesus, his primary/beloved community, but he was always walking. And that is what the Old Man did. Followed in his footsteps. According to legend of the Catholic Church, John was the only apostle not to have been martyred, who died of natural causes in Ephesus and was buried there. The Old Man, I think, took his place and walked on.

Diotrophes: I'm not saying Diotrophes didn't walk. I am sure he started out walking, or maybe he didn't walk. Maybe he was just one of the beloved people in the beloved community of St. John, like the Old Man—a second generation, disciple of the disciple. But Diotrophes got to thinking someone should stay and mind the sheep at the home base. I am thinking, given the designation of the Elder as the elder or the Old Man, that it is more likely that Diotrophes was a disciple of the Old Man, a kind of third generation. If John died in 99 CE, (which is close enough to right) and the Old Man, being a young man when he started walking with John is probably, like fifty when John dies and he takes over his rounds and Diotrophes, having a very Greek name, and Ephesus being a predominantly

Greek city, was probably brought into the fold there and didn't follow John from Jerusalem, like the Old Man did. He probably was not even around when the apostle John was, so at the time of the Old Man's writing he was a young upstart, a rising star in the community. I am thinking—maybe because I've made so many rounds though this Readers Gift Bible—that a beloved line can be drawn. In the Gospel of John, John makes reference to, *the beloved disciple*, which most scholars assume is self-referential. John is Jesus's beloved disciple. The Old Man is the beloved disciple of the beloved disciple and Diotrophes is the beloved disciple of the Old Man—at one time. But here in the third generation, things fall apart. The center cannot hold. Intrigue. Church history records that Diotrophes goes on to take on the title of Bishop and is said to have been a key figure in institutionalizing the liturgical hierarchy of Bishop, Pryspeter and Deacon.

Gaius: A contemporary of the Old Man's, of the second generation of walkers. He was baptized by Paul, First Corinthians tells us this, and that Gauis stayed with Paul while he wrote the Epistle to the Romans. Gauis walked with the apostle Paul all over Asia Minor and after Paul's death joined the beloved community in Ephesus. By the time the Old Man is writing to Gauis, he is himself an old man, presumably an old and trusted friend and certainly well respected by all. This could explain why the Old Man sends Demetrius to Gauis, believing that Diotrophes would not dare expel a former companion of the apostle Paul's for receiving a friend of his. I cannot help noting, additionally that Gauis is also the name shared by the Roman Emperor of fifty years previous, Gaius Caesar Augustus Germanicus, more popularly known as Caligula. Gaius Caligula began as a true friend of the Roman people and the senate, handing out pardons and bonuses to the soldiers and justice to the citizens only to be murdered by his own people three short years later for his duplicity and extreme self serving (if not insane) actions. I don't think I trust Gaius.

Demetrius: Based on internal evidence from the text, Demetrius was the Old Man's most trusted protégé, given that he is the Old Man's choice for this delicate mission. He is of the third generation and possibly has taken the place that Diotrophes once held in the Old Man's regard. As to how he fairs in history and how his mission turns out, I seem to have some memory of a Demetrius the Deacon who was martyred in Thessalonica some years later. Possibly indicating that he eventually joined with those who sought to institutionalize the church—Diotrophes. He was one of the early saints of the church—his ring and his *orarium* (neck scarf) having been dipped in his blood and preserved. The relics were lost but found in the ruins of a church dedicated to him. The discoverer, having suffered from childhood with a clubbed foot was immediately healed on touching them. A cult grew up around St. Demetrius and his relics were said to have healed thousands. That doesn't seem like the kind of thing the Old Man would approve of.

I capped the Uni-ball and turned back to the Juanitos to read. I waited until after ten thirty to make sure everyone had left. The last study classes and team meeting ended at eight thirty, but people lingered. Mostly, the lingering was what they came for, so I waited until ten thirty to be sure. I slowly put on my suit coat, picked up my bag, slid the Bible into it and moved on the balls of my feet. I nestled my office door shut behind me, locked it with the quiet little click, and went straight to the food pantry where people came on Wednesdays at noon and Fridays from four to six to pick up donated items. I found a big box full of canned goods and post-expiration date bread and English muffins. "This will be perfect," I thought and dumped the contents of the box onto the stainless steel counter. This was a good solid box, reinforced bottom and punch out handles on the sides. I set off to ransack the library and the offices of my colleagues for any books that might help my project.

Chapter 3

The Edge Of Fear… Dark God… Pastor Bob
Wickman's Daughter… Praise Team Stool…
"Hello?" ....

I had waited so long for everyone to leave, had gone
over my plans so many times in my head, was so oc-
cupied with my tasks, that when I left the pantry I
was surprised to find myself alone in a dark hallway
in an empty building. An empty church building is
more empty than other empty buildings. It ranks far
above being in your grade school after school is out.
It's a place you know so well, are there for hours a day,
but being there at an irregular time feels strange and
forbidden. Like seeing a teacher smoking, or the jani-
tor talking to the librarian, leaning in close.

A church is even stranger. People are supposed to
be there. Oh, and God. Some suspicion or promise or
hope that God might be there. Which I think is the
main reason for the weirdness. On an unconscious
level there is the understanding that if the spirit of
God is there with the lights on, when the lights are
off other darker spirits must come out. Or, really that
God might actually be there in the dark. And whatever

position one holds about the benevolence of God, no one wants to meet God alone in the dark. It's not weirdness; it's the edge of fear.

Everyone was gone. I could feel the emptiness, and in the emptiness some dark presence just beyond the breathing of the air conditioning. I tried to listen through it, to find the sounds of that thing moving. I held the box to my chest by the handles and walked. I navigated the halls by Exit light. I kept thinking I heard that thing, so I kept stopping to listen. I would stop and the sound would stop. Did I hear me walking, echoing off the hard surfaces of floor and walls? I started walking again, and I would hear the thing again. I could see it in my mind as a shadow cast by nothing, just the legs and feet creeping forward in long steps, knees coming up high, hands reaching forward. I stopped again, and the sound stopped. Once you let the primordial, little-kid-scared-of-the-dark demon in just a little bit, it follows you around all night.

The shortest way to the offices was through the sanctuary, the dark God epicenter of a dark church. I can turn the lights on in the offices when I get there, that seems safe, but I can't set this enormous space ablaze in the middle of the night. There are windows, big windows—it would be seen from the freeway and across the freeway at the Gasateria. I actually don't even know how to turn on the sanctuary lights. There must be a switch or some big thing you throw—which I guess is called a switch. I don't even know where it would be. I heard something over my shoulder. Which was ridiculous and I knew it and I told myself—but I also told myself that the darkness is complete and someone, something, could be leaning up against the wall right next to me holding its breath. I did a little jog run, trying to keep the box and my bag from bouncing into my body and making noise. Why did I need to be quiet? The thing was the one trying to sneak up on me? This thought made me try to run quieter and faster. There was no more hall around me now—I could feel the open space. The walls were gone. I was in the gathering area, the vestibule outside the sanctuary. I start walking. I put my left hand, straight arm in front of me until I found the sanctuary door.

Inside the sanctuary it was outer space, but with no stars or sun to reflect off the big blue ball. Nothing but darkness and expanse. Of course there was some dark Thing in here, all darkness is present—I wish the ceiling were lower and the walls closer. I step forward not convinced that there is floor in front of me. A drop-off into the abyss seems more likely. I don't think I could deal with tumbling into the abyss. It is not the fall that scares me. It's just the tumbling. Silent scream tumbling. I want to reach my hand out for the end of the pews to guide me down the aisles, but I don't want that ghostly long-fingered hand to clamp down on top of mine and hold me there. So I hold my box close and bump softly, occasionally into them with my knees. I am almost paralyzed by the sudden thought of someone running at me silently in the darkness, slamming into my body, not even being able to see him until after I feel him twisting the knife in my gut. I waited for almost half a minute: nothing. I put my hand on my stomach to check for bleeding. I move forward. Okay, this time I really had heard something. There was someone moving behind me. I quicken my tentative steps. I am not going to stop any more and listen because I know by now it is just the sound of my own movements. But, then I heard labored breathing and I heard him knock into a pew and grunt irritatedly. I moved faster, forgetting to be quiet. He knew I was here. He was following me. My box hit something hard and the edges cut into my chest. I felt the wall, found the door. I was at the front of the sanctuary. I pushed it open quickly and forced it closed, fighting the hydraulics. I dropped the box and pulled out my keys, fingering them until I felt the master key, palm rubbing the door until I found the lock, put the key in and turned. I waited. I listened. I put my ear to the door. Nothing. I was insane. A scared little kid. Nothing. No one.

I was in the hallway to the offices. The night-lights

of the parking lot came through the window at the end of the hall. I could see the row of office doors. I was fine. I was back to earth. I smiled at my scare and walked normally. Then I thought of the Old Man. I could see him like a memory, knocking into the end of a pew in the dark, grunting irritatedly and rubbing his leg. See him feeling his way to the door at the front of the sanctuary and finding it locked. I walked somewhat less normally.

I didn't really expect to find much, but still I was disappointed. I did find Bultman's commentary on the Epistles of John in Stan Paulson's office (everyone refers to him only as Our Senior Pastor), which pleased and surprised me. I also took three packs of cinnamon gum from his desk drawer.

I got an Anchor Bible commentary on the Juanito's from Bob Wickman's office. Anchor Commentaries are usually pretty good for translation and textual questions—but not for any big ideas. Plus, I took a picture of his daughter on a merry-go-round horse looking scared. What was wrong with me? Stealing things from my colleagues' offices made me happy. And somehow, the state I was in made it seem like the right thing to do. I tell myself that it is helpful for Pastor Bob Wickman to come into his office as he has done six days a week for the last nine years and realize that the picture of his scared-looking daughter is missing. It will interrupt his life and he will have to think, "Didn't I have a picture of my daughter on the desk?" And he will think of his daughter and miss her and leave work early and go home to be with her.

I was seized by a sudden realization. Pastor Bob Wickman does not have a daughter. I looked around, suddenly feeling like there must be cameras in the room hidden in the bookshelves or behind a plant. This was bait. The picture of an unknown little girl sitting on a merry-go-round pony looking scared. Is this part of some psychological evaluation? Have they placed various items in the room to see which ones I would choose to steal? What does it mean that I took the picture and not the letter opener? I looked into the box. Hold on. I was letting myself go. I was letting myself go too far. My attorney was right; pretending I wasn't thinking what I was thinking was not mental heath. I had to let go of something, part of my stability project, to embark on my Juanitos project. But—screaming up from the inside of my rib cage—I cannot let go completely. Letting go completely would jeopardize the project. It was ridiculous to think that there were cameras and there was a test. How would they have known that I was going to go around stealing various books and items from staff offices? I didn't even know I was going to do it. I'm letting go too much. Abandoning stability altogether. I have to think of

the project. I have a lot more work to do. Maintain. Maintenance and utility. I took the letter opener and headed for the library.

The library was worse than the offices. There were hardly any books. It was videos, DVDs and computer software and teenage Christian culture magazines. I looked around for the oldest and most unused looking book I could find. *The Wisdom of the Ancient Rabbis: A Midrash Reader.* Well there is something I know nothing about. I threw it in the box and headed for the utility closet.

I was moving in. Getting things set up. One by one I was taking the cleaning supplies off the shelves and replacing them with the books I had scavenged. I cleared off the workbench and took a stool from the Praise Team rehearsal space. It would be a fine desk.

I sat down on the praise team stool. My muscles relaxed a little, enough only to realize I had been tensing them. My heart rate began to slow to the same effect. Something was happening to me. I felt dizzy or lost. I felt hot. I knew hot was coming.

It's hot. And he's getting old. Everything slows down in the heat. I can feel him. I can see him. The Old Man is talking to me.

He feels humiliated by the pen, the black ink staining his hands and the papyrus he's writing on. His forehead is streaked but he doesn't yet know it.

"These letters were the compromise." I start—my head jumping from droop to stare straight ahead when he speaks. "It wasn't supposed to go any further than that."

He is old and things are changing. He feels sad but also furious. His rage won't come until after the sun goes down and the day cools off. His body can't produce the rage in this kind of heat. Lethargy, depression, sadness and an unknown quantity of unacknowledged self-pity is all his decrepitude allows him.

It's maybe not that nice to call him the Old Man. Elder or old man—the Greek doesn't distinguish. I don't mean any disrespect. It is just that I want to know him and I want to love him and I want to shake his skinny body of work upside down by the ankles until he gives it up. Gives up the meaning and lets me in on the joke. Makes Jesus tell me why the hell the Old Man and his skinny little epistle missiles made the cut. I try to taste the air, to see the utility closet.

"Hey, Old Man, Old Man? I don't mean any disrespect it's just…. Are you hot? I am so hot. Do you need something?" He isn't looking good at all; what the hell time is it? My throat burns and it wants to come back up on me but the flush is spreading, had spread and sweat is starting to bead on the high part of my forehead way past where my hair used to cover. It must be later now, much later than I thought, but it hasn't cooled. The sun is still squinting almost horizontal through the window. Two-foot-thick mud brick walls. The roof is mud and sticks it looks like. They must have a surplus of mud. Seems like the mud should be cooler. Just this room and another past it. In here a table, low. He sits on the floor, scrolls all around on the desk and the ground. He rubs his forehead and then notices the ink on his hand. He wipes his forehead with his other hand, diluting the ink streak with the sweat. He looks at both his hands, fingers—palm side first then the back and back again. The fingers on the right deeply ink stained and wet. The right only with the ink slurry he picked up from his forehead. This all starts to deflate him until it must occur to him what his forehead must look like and he grunts out an involuntary laugh. And then he is wiping his forehead with the flats of his fingertips, looking at them and then he looks at me half smiling, "This is what I have come to. It's all I can do, write these letters and hope. They won't even listen to me." He looks at me. I feel bad for locking him in the sanctuary. He breathes. He raised his eyebrows, indicating: Well? What is this about? I mash my lips together and lean forward slightly, nodding, indicating: Oh yeah, right. Where do I start?

Yeah, where do I start? I have the Old Man, the Elder, right here. I can just ask, ask him what he knows.

I want to be careful because he does seem a little left of the dial, vigor wise. I don't want to upset him, but I can see through his eyes and into the heart of the factory and it is clockwork efficiency. I have some very specific questions, and as I am working out how to finesse the situation a women comes into the room with a big clay pitcher and some clean low-ball tumblers. She picks up an empty pitcher, looks in it, and then looks at us disapprovingly. "I just got here," I said, but she doesn't let me off the hook. The Old Man smiles at her. She touches him on the shoulder as she leaves.

It is casual but reveals something—I don't know what. I couldn't get clear what the relationship is. Daughter? Wife? She isn't as old as he is, but she isn't young. I am having a hard time getting clear.

"This is her house. I stay here," he says.

"Oh." I say. And then because I can't think of anything to say and because I'm not sure what this situation is I say, "I was doing pretty well until he set me off, my attorney," as a way of explaining my presence to the Old Man. "I mean I wasn't exactly taking all my prescriptions in all the prescribed ways, but I was functioning pretty much without visions or obsessions or speaking or rarely even thinking about Molotov cocktails or fires. I practically didn't long for the destruction of anything."

I don't want to alarm the old guy, and I realize that

what I am saying could seem odd. I want to change the subject. He picks up his pen up off the makeshift desk. "Face to face, mouth to mouth, that's how this thing need to be said," he mutters and leaves.

The sun dance was the major communal religious ceremony for many tribes of Plains Indians whose bison-hunting culture flourished during the 18th and 19th centuries. The rite celebrates renewal—the spiritual rebirth of the participant and his people, as well as the regeneration of the living Earth with all its components. The ritual, involving sacrifice and supplication to ensure harmony between all living beings, continues to be practiced by many contemporary Native Americans.

The most renowned priest was also the best lodge maker. He ran the entire ceremony and would instruct the participant in building a preparatory tepee. He would choose a tall, straight tree to use as the sun pole, which serves as the center of the sun dance. It becomes the center of the universe and the place where the dancer meets the great spirit. Sacred objects are collected, such as brush, buffalo hide, long straws with tobacco in them and other religious objects. They are placed in a bundle and tied near the top of the sun pole.

Who knows how to give what is needed? How to give just enough, but not too much. Enough—a paper torn from a twenty-year-old magazine that says, "I know who you are and I like you." That is not too much, but it is all one needs.

After my "crisis" our Senior Pastor suggested that I spend some time in the in-patient program at Maple Lakes Regional Community Hospital. I remember agreeing with him that it seemed like a good idea. But I cannot recall if I remember agreeing with him because all you can do is agree with him, and I had a mortgage and still owed thirty-seven thousand eight hundred dollars on my student loans—or because I actually agreed with him, that something was not completely right with me and that I should take any help that was offered. What I do remember is that Amy, the Assistant to the Administrative Assistant to our Senior Pastor and *a personal friend of mine*, did what she always did. She made the gesture that reminded me it is "O.K., after all to be human." As I walked past her with our Senior Pastor, who was taking the time personally to drive me to MLRCH, she shook my hand and passed me a note. After I had been admitted (is that like confessing) and taken to my room I took the note out of my pocket and unfolded it. On a scrap of printer paper, in a hurried hand, with a blue ballpoint pen she had scribbled "Soylent Green is people!"

The Hallmark envelope with the Sun Dance article came two days later.

All I had left to do now was go on my supply run and get back here before people started showing up for work at seven. Then I would return to the sub-basement utility closet and stay here until I answer the question Idiot John gave me. Where was I going to get a cot at four in the morning? I might have to figure out some other sleeping arrangements. I grabbed my coat, put my Mead in my bag and opened the door of the utility closet. I almost tripped over it. A fax machine. Just outside the door of my bunker someone had placed a fax machine. At four in the morning. The Old Man? No, he didn't use the door when he left. A long phone cord came out the back and traveled along the wall to the telephone demarcation box. The front panel had been removed and the cord spliced in to one of the lines. I looked right, trying to see through the boiler and the ductwork. I looked left, the forced air kicked on. I picked up the fax machine, there was plenty of extra cord, I brought it into the closet and shut the door. There was easily enough space under it for the cord. I set it on the workbench, plugged it into one of the four wall sockets and picked up the receiver. "Hello," a voice said.

Chapter 4

Gaseteria… Batman… Ordo Praedictorum…
Psycho-Spiritual… Whiplash… "Go, Go, Go"…
"Hello?"…………………………………………………………………………

A rote human interaction can momentarily trigger
sanity. Or humanity. It is a beautiful and hardwired
thing. Human beings respond to other human beings
as a first instinct. If being robbed at gunpoint, the best
response to "Give me your money, now!" is the pleasant but slightly impatient question, "What time is it?"

The dangerous and imposing figure will without
conscious thought sense both your urgency and desire
to help him if you have the time, look at his watch and
tell you, "Ten after ten." At which point you say, "Oh,
man, I'm sorry, I'm so late," as you jog off. Of course
he may shoot you without giving you the time. Human beings are somewhat unpredictable.

I was someplace between looking at my watch and
a gun going off in my hand. I squeezed the receiver
tighter and pulled it back from my head six inches.

"Listen to me," the voice said. "This is quite important. I need you to pick me up on the frontage
road near the gas station. It's beginning to rain, hurry."

53

He hung up. He hung up?

I patted my bag to make sure the Mead and my keys were in it, skipped over the fax machine cord out the door and up the stairs. Moving fast but not running, aware of the demon darkness but not at a panic level, more concentrating on getting to the car and getting to the Gaseteria to pick up…. Yeah. O.K. His "hello" had triggered an involuntary "hello" from me, granting me a fog-clearing, reality-reentering moment. I could have so easily been completely overcome by panic. A full-scale freak out. I mean, the fax machine, the voice on the other end. But instead I'd just headed for my car to pick up…. Wait, here it was: Was I the one with the gun? Or was he? I stopped for a minute to think. Then I decided to keep moving and think.

Guy with a gun says, "Give me your money, now!" I say, "What time is it?" He responds automatically, "Ten after ten." And I jog off. I am right now, jogging off. But I am jogging off because He said, "Come and pick me up." Which is equivalent to his saying, "What time is it?" Which would make him the muggee. In spite of the fact that I am right now jogging off. I am, in fact, jogging off because he said, "What time is it?" Which makes me the guy with the gun. Furthermore, he said, "hello" first, which prompted my automatic "Hello" which again makes me the guy with the gun.

But I don't feel like the guy with the gun.

I push through the door out onto the parking lot. It was raining. Heavily. Pulling out of my parking space it was hard to see; the windshield wipers were doing their best, but not keeping up. I was trying to clear books and trash off the passenger seat for him. I almost lost control shoving a wadded fast food bag and an empty pack of cigarettes under the seat. I turned on to Maple Quarry Road, and then right onto the frontage road. Not the frontage road that the Gaseteria is on but the one that runs behind the church. I had to drive down to Cedar Quarry Trail and cross the freeway so I was heading in the right direction on the one-way frontage road to get to the Gaseteria.

The rain was sheeting down, the car was driving in the right direction, the passenger seat cleared of most debris, and I was teetering on the edge of control. I'm teetering. The clear, commanding instructions set me straight, but this pounding rain was pushing back the clarity, pounding it back. I was driving forward. I could see through the window-warping rain the liquid lights of the Gaseteria complex and on the road near it a crazy giant in a Batman costume, scissoring his arms over his head, like he was trying to fly or flag down a train. Me. No, Batman was flagging me down. Without a thought or a question I pulled over. Batman ran to the car, his cape too soaked to unfurl behind him. I reached to unlock the door as he pulled up the handle. We both paused. I reached to unlock the door again as he pulled up the handle. "You have to wait until I unlock it," I yelled at Batman through the window glass. "It won't work if you are pulling on it when I am trying to unlock it."

"What?"

"Don't pull on the handle." I pulled on the lock. He grabbed the handle. Stall. I hit the door in frustration. Batman backed away. I opened the door from the inside and pushed it open.

He sort of shook off outside and then jumped into the car, his knees folded too tightly against the dash. He fumbled around the base of the seat, front and sides looking for the "slide back the seat" thing. "It's on the right side, way back," I told him. Rain was blowing in. He found it and slid the seat all the way back, pulled his cape over his lap, slammed the door and said, "Right, thanks. If you could just drive somewhere out of the rain. I can't think. D'you know what I mean?"

I did know what he meant, but didn't say so. I looked around. I drove to the car wash stall in the back of the Gaseteria. I found the receipt in the glove compartment, which involved asking Batman to squish his knees against the door so I could get it open.

"I have a code from the last time I got gas but the line was too long."

"Oh," he said.

I punched in the code, the garage door opened and I pulled in until the red light flashed. The car wash started up—spraying and soaping and mopping and rinsing. Touchless?

In a matter of fact way he said, "This isn't much better. It is actually worse."

"Just wait till it's done. It's only the basic wash." I yelled.

He smiled and nodded. I looked down at his boots while he stared ahead pleasantly as the various swoshing and spraying went on. The boots came up almost knee high over leather pants; I could see a studded belt where the cape had fallen away. He was wearing a comparatively ordinary black shirt with a sort of white thing at the neck. His hair was black, cut in that short roman way. This was an expensive Batman costume, but not very accurate. He wrapped the long black cape over his body. The rinse jets trickled to an end, and the green go sign flashed. I didn't go.

"That's a pretty nice cape," I said, still looking him up and down.

"It is not a cape exactly. It is a cappa, a black friar's cloak." My eyes fell on the white strip at his neck. He lifted his chin up to help. "Yes," he said, "Ordo Praedicatorum, Order of Preachers, a Dominican Friar and priest."

"Oh," I said looking at his boots and leather pants.

"I have a story to tell you. I think it will help."

"Help what?" I was so far from my bunker. He turned his body sideways in the seat to face me and patted my leg and smiled. "May I begin?"

I looked straight ahead at the green light flashing go, go, go.

"There had long been rumors throughout the Decapolis and the surrounding region that in Gerasa they had created a monster."

"The Decapolis?"

"The Decapolis are the ten predominately Greek cities in the region of Palestine in the first century."

"I know what the Decapolis is. It just seems really odd that a leather boy black friar would call me up at three in the morning and ask me to pick him up in the rain so he could tell me a story about a monster in the region of the Decapolis."

"Yes, well, he said it would help you in your…calling….or did he say mission?"

"Project. I am calling it a project, and how do you know Idiot John?"

"Idiot who? I'd watch how you, uh, you know 'those in glass houses….' May I continue?"

Go. Go. Go.

"Gerasa was a city in ruin and constant turmoil. Its history was of one attack after another. The city was nearly destroyed when the King of Judah laid siege and captured the city but did not care to hold it. He appointed a legion of his army to stay and make their home there, but it was merely a gesture in the city of more than ten thousand. It wasn't so much an occupation as a presence. The inhabitants of Gerasa were left mostly unharmed and allowed to rebuild, but the legion of Jewish soldiers destined to always be in the minority were never quite at ease. Eventually many of them took wives and had children, but even after several generations of intermarrying a rift remained between those who could trace their fathers back to the original Jewish legion and those whose fathers were among the gentile citizens of Gerasa at the time of the siege. Although it became harder and harder to tell which was which. Some say the situation was made worse because the city was made up of people who had only known war and violence. So, that even in the relative times of peace small disputes often escalated into bloodshed. And further retaliation for the bloodshed resulted from the small disputes.

"Gerasa was such a violent and unsafe place that travelers and traders would avoid it, leading to poverty and, as poverty always does, further violence.

"Then, it is said, the rabbi of the small synagogue and the high priest of the massive Temple of Diana met in secret to devise a plan to bring peace to the city.

"Calling on a deep and ancient magic from before

the time that either of the holy men knew, they set out to make a Golem—a manlike creature without a soul. Many ancient mythologies tell stories of the attempts of men to create life. In the near east the creatures are made from mud. In Norse mythology from the burls of trees. The two holy men would make their Golem from the soil mixed with seawater and bring it to the temple of Diana, the goddess of nature and through incantations and rituals and prayers that are lost to us now, would appeal to the goddess to reward their efforts and bring life to the Golem and peace to the city.

"The plan was this: The heads of every household in the city would gather in the temple and through these rituals and prayers and incantations every man would transfer the dark side of their souls, and their household's souls, into the Golem. It was then believed that having no more darkness, no more treachery, no more violence, no more sin left in their souls they could live in peace as brothers and neighbors.

"When the chanting and the prayers of all the men in the city had come to an end and the last echo of the final prayer had faded, when the smoke cleared from the fires of the sacrifices and the incense burned out, all was still. All was quiet and they raised their heads to look on the altar where the Golem had been laid. They saw standing there a man, or what appeared to be a man—shaking and with the look of a deranged question on his face, contorted, both afraid and ready to strike.

"It was believed that the dark side of the soul of every man there had come together in the Golem to give him life—but it was half a life. He was only half alive. For though many men gave him half of their souls, the Golem possessed, still, only half a soul. He could not speak, but grunt and wail and spit. It was thought that he could not reason, nor understand. The stillness and silence was broken by the men charging the Golem with the chains they had prepared. They bound him in shackles and in irons and burned into his forehead with a hot poker the name Hamartia, which means sin. They led him outside of the city to the tombs where they chained him. They called him Sin, for he carried the spirits of all the evil of the city. The goddess of nature had heard their prayers and granted them a gift. But like nature, her gifts are sometimes beautiful and sometimes destructive—and always uncontrollable.

"From that time on when a dispute arose among the men in the city, the two at odds would go out to the tombs with the elders and they would together beat Golem until they were exhausted, their rage spent, then sit down and form a compromise. When a boy in Gerasa came of age he would hunt down Golem with the men of his household (for the demoniac Hamartia was always breaking out of his chains, though he never left the land of the tombs) and he would hurl stones until the Golem could not stand. In that way the boy was assured that sin and darkness were purged from his soul. When the harvest was small, trade was slow or the rains didn't come, the men of Gerasa would go to the edge of the tombs and throw torches at Hamartia in an attempt to set him on fire.

"During a time of relative peace, Jesus came to the region of the Decapolis, from the other side, across the sea…"

"Wait, that is the end of the story? That will help me?"

Batman raised his brows, a little put off, "I am, you might have noticed, still telling the story."

"No, you switched to a Jesus story."

"I am still telling the same story."

"How does Jesus fit in?"

"Jesus fits it quite well, I think you will find if you listen to the story." He cocked his head, raised his brows and smiled. And waited, I guess to see if I would say anything else. So, I didn't .

He began again, "During a time of relative peace, brought about by Hamartia the Golem, Jesus came to the region of the Decapolis from across the sea, which was called the mystery of God, because only the divine can control the sea or understands its ways.

Sometimes the sea gives food and plenty, other times destruction and death, and no one knows when or why. Know one knows what is in its depths but God, so it is thought that it must hold all the mysteries of God.

"When Jesus stepped out of the boat, immediately a man from the tombs filled with unclean spirits met him. When the Golem saw Jesus from a distance, he ran to him and bowed down and then a loud, tormented voice broke through his grunts and wails and for the first time he spoke these anguished words: 'What have you to do with me, Jesus, Son of the Most High God? I beg you by God not to torment me.'

"Jesus matching his volume replied, 'Come out of the man, you unclean spirits!' And then in a lower voice asked him, 'What is your name?'

"'I am Hamartia,' said Golem, 'The sins of many.'

"The Sin of the Gerasa begged Jesus earnestly not to send him out of the creature of mud. There was a great herd of swine feeding on the hillside and Hamartia begged him, 'Send us into the swine, let us enter them.'

"So he gave the permission and the dark, half souls of the people of Gerasa left Hamartia and entered the swine, and the herd, numbering about two thousand, rushed down the steep bank into the sea and was swallowed up by the mystery of God.

"Some of the men from the city who tended the

swine herd ran off and reported to everyone what had happened. Then many men rushed out to see what had happened. Running, out of breath, and talking—what will become of them with out the Golem?

"When they reached Jesus they didn't find the lifeless mixture of soil and seawater the holy men had used to form the Golem, but a man sitting there clothed and in his right mind—not only alive, but fully alive. Not at all the half alive creature they had created, but a man abundantly alive. When the men of the city saw this they were afraid, and they begged Jesus to leave their land at once.

"Jesus did not answer them but quoted to them from the book of Isaiah: 'I was ready to be sought out by those who did not ask, to be found by those who did not seek me. I said, Here I am, here I am, to a nation that did not call on my name. I held out my hands all day long to a rebellious people, who walk in a way that is not good, following their own devices; a people who provoke me to my face continually, sacrificing in gardens and offering incense on bricks, who sit inside tombs and spend the night in secret places; who eat swine's flesh with broth of abominable things in their vessels.'

"And then he turned to get in the boat, Golem stopped him and begged Jesus to take him. But Jesus refused and said to him, 'Go with your friends,' referring to the men from the city, 'and tell them how much the Lord has done for you, and what mercy he has shown you.'

"And Golem went to the city and began to proclaim what Jesus had done for him. And all around the city of Gerasa men encountered their sin, on the streets and in the market, and their sin proclaimed to them the Mercy of God. And all were amazed."

We sat. I had a slow realization that his hand had been taping my leg rhythmically as he told the story and had now stopped.

I sat there. I looked down at my leg. I looked at Batman. "What?" I asked. "What? The Golem and the Gospel?" I was moving in and out. On the border between asking myself— with the collected composure of the Man of Pure Reason—in what way exactly did this piece fit into the puzzle of my Juanitos project and having the terrifying realization that I was sitting in a carwash in the middle of the night with the Black Friar Batman, listening to some extra-gospelar tale of a man of mud—*and almost taking it seriously*. If I tilted my head to the left, something in my brain rolled to that side and I became the Man of Pure Reason. If I tilted my head the right—toward Batman—that little thing went skeetering to the other side and I could see what an absolute round-the-bend-psychic-break-in-the-works I am. Right: skeet, skeet, skeet, clink! How very intriguing your tale is. Are you saying there is some correlation between my project and....Left: skeet, skeet, skeet, skeet, clunk! I Am Losing My Mind! So, I try to hold my head perfectly level, neck stiff, and avoid that psycho-spiritual whiplash. I've got to keep that little ball in the middle.

Batman was patient, seemingly aware of what I was going through and wanted to let me work things out on my own. So when I stopped furrowing and unfurrowing my brow and my pupils stopped shrinking and growing with insight and horror and focussed on him from my new balanced position, he smiled simply and gave me a slight bow of his head, indicating, "There we are now. See you're just fine. Now is there anything else I can do for you?"

I felt pain in my left leg. I had had my foot on the clutch the entire time. I took it off, the car, still running, lurched forward and died. The flashing "Go" sign turned to "Thank you, thank you, thank you" and the big garage door in front of us rolled open. He opened the car door and got out, ducked his head back in, and said, "Follow the victim."

"What?" He shut the door, and as he walked away he triggered the giant blow dryers, which unfurled his cape behind him as he left the car wash bay.

Fast. I was driving too fast. The rain, was not falling anymore but the streets were slickish and I was in third gear, no, damn, second. I needed fourth. There. Yeah, too fast. I needed to go home and call the whole thing off. It was too much. I cursed my attorney for whatever kind of delayed-action hallucinogen he'd slipped me at T. J. O'Tooles. I needed to find my driveway and get home and in my bed. Yes, all the driveways were presenting themselves, flourishing themselves before me, offering themselves to me. Pick me, they tantalized, but I knew they were not mine. I was tempted. As I approached, each driveway undulated toward me like a wave with some unique flourish at the end by the mailbox. But I knew, 'you are not my driveway.' There was my driveway. It did nothing. Just remained a driveway. I pulled in, punched the garage door opener, and it uncoiled to seal me in. I stumbleed through the door, the kitchen, the hallway, the open bedroom door, found the corner of the bed with my hand in the dark, traced it to the top and laid my self down.

Flat on my back, relieved. Head not spinning, no ball skeetering, but full and pushing out in every way. I inhaled. She patted the bed, progressively searching for my hand. She found it, rubbed it back and forth three soft times and then, giving it a squeeze, sighed and rolled over.

I laid there for a full minute, trying to remember if there was something really important about my life that I could have forgotten, counting one-Mississippi, two-Mississippi…

I sat straight up, got out of bed, and left. I could remember what I'd forgotten later. Now I had to go. Follow the victim. Follow the victim. Back to the bunker. I'd never looked at my Mead. I was back at the church and I had nothing on the list. It didn't matter. More light? A lamp, a cot? I was not going to sleep and more light would not help me see. I needed to talk to Idiot John.

Chapter 5

Drilling into a two-inch thick metal door with a slow
drill and a dull bit is much harder than I thought. It
takes a lot of forward thrust to drill eight holes: four
on the utility closet door and four on the jamb.

When I got back to the church, I didn't want to
go in the main doors by the office, so I parked my
car near the back of the parking lot and skirted the
flood-lit center. I had never known of any kind of
back door, but obviously with a building of this size
there has to be more ways to enter it than through
the obvious big glass doors. There must be any number of side and back and service entrance doors. But
there's no sidewalk leading around the back of the
church. Only landscaped lawn sloping away from the
building, obviously for drainage purposes. *Obviously*
because I am walking at the base of the sloping and
the grass is sponging with the runoff from all the rain.
Soaking through my shoes and wicking up my pant
legs. I am slipping in muddy grass garnished with fat

earthworms trying to avoid drowning. At the back of the building I see, four doors spaced unevenly along its expanse. Trying to calculate where each one will bring me into the church, I pick the third from the end. My key works, the door opened right near my stairwell to the basement. I sloshed down it, and then the next set to the sub-basement.

It was a great comfort to return to the relative safety of my closet after being outside with the weather and superhero priests and undulating driveways and . . . sometimes I remember to forget. My comfort (relative as my safety) was short lived. I was stopped halfway between the stairs and the bunker by a sensation of difference. That is, not a sensation that I was different but that somehow something in my surroundings had changed. I slowly pivot… and I cannot say if I had *missed* the hallways on either side of the stairs or if, well… it is probably not possible that they were not there before, but I will say that I did not see them before.

Whether I had overlooked the hallways or they had recently appeared, it is a terrifying and thrilling thing to see the safe, even comfortable, familiarity of a physical space in a completely different way—to see here in this place that which could not be seen before. The terror and the thrill increased with the next thought—where do those halls lead? Ink-a-bink,

HE DRILLED INTO THE DOOR

I start with the one on the left of the stairs, closest to the storage room door.

I reach inside the dark hall and flip the switch; ancient fluorescents buzz and sputter. The light is brown and dim. Submarine light. The walls and ceiling are two inch by four inch pale yellow tiles. This is an old underground subway station, "Damn you! Damn you all to hell!" Or it led from the old locker room to the old pool. But really it only led back about sixteen feet, turns to the right, continues on for another ten feet and turns to the right again. After another sixteen feet I come out on the other side of the stairs. Enter on the left, return on the right—stairs stay put, in the middle.

Again I turn to head for my bunker when I see the residue of a presence. I am not the only one how has slogged through the mud outside. At the base of the stairs, muddy, puddley foot prints heading down the left hallway. Idiot John? Or some other flesh and blood apparition? Despite my better judgment, I follow the footsteps. Well, I have no better judgment; I have no judgment other than that which I reserve for myself. I follow slowly, trying not to squeak in the submarine hall. I track this tracker, who, I am sure is, following me. Like the Old Man. I turn the first right. Was this the Black Friar returning to share something more with me? "Follow the victim," Is he following me? Am I the victim? I make the last right and see the light from the end of the hall. Whoever is following me is waiting for me beyond the corner. Except, "waiting?" I am beyond thinking that someone will hit me on the head with a pipe-ish sort of thing when I step out of the hall. Or I wish someone would hit me on the head with that kind of thing when I step around the corner. So I step. But no violence. Nobody. Silence. Emptiness. That is when I notice that someone has joined my pursuer. There is a second set of muddy, puddley footprints. I wish Christopher Robin were here to give me a "silly old bear," and make everything alright. Completely convinced I'd been chasing my own shadow, I head for the utility closet and then think, "They want me to think I am chasing my shadow, right?" So, I look at the storage closet and pull out my key. Instinct, perhaps? Some kind of instinct that what I need to protect me will be in there.

I unlock it and on opening realize it is not a closet at all. The sign on the door says, "storage". I implied closet" on my own. I have to read closer. Just read what is written.

Storage.

Sto[rage]. Really?

It is a room.

Large and full, jumbled, beautiful, dusty with heavy black dust. And so much stuff.

Janitors, or physical plant specialists, are the

cerebral cortex of any institution. They know how to make things function. They know everything that happens, that has happened, that is to happen. They are the chief priests, the rabbis, the physicians, the historians. They are the keepers of the institution's narratives, histories told in physical archives. With every remodel and expansion, they save something. When the old classrooms are turned in to offices and the windows were updated, they stored the old windows down here, and if not the windows, then the crank handles used to open them. Because not all the windows were updated, and if a crank handle should break . . . and even if they were updated who throws away perfectly good crank handles. New doors—save the hinges, knobs and locksets. Old light fixtures, carpet, signs. You could trace the growth—the lean times through the layers of what was stored. What was once central, what was presumed lost. It's all down here, one narrative or commentary or counter commentary stacked against the other. The decades are debated through the collection of old signs. The stoic lettering of the original, the seventies updates, the sleek sans serif of the eighties, the faux updated original lettering from the nineties.

It is all here in storage. This is nothing like the maintaince shop up one level. There the purpose is to main*tain*. I am no longer able to be about that shop. There it is full of new battery powered tools and handlights and zip saws, compartments and shelves and lighting. All to help maintain. Here, just piles and stacks of meaning and history.

My instincts were right. It's what I need, this storage room. I find a never-been-used padlock with keys still in the packaging, a hasp set, an old drill with frayed electrical tape winding off the cord, a metal bit and bolts, and wrenches. All the things I need to do the job.

I gather them all in a canvas bag and grab a tarnished brass chalice from some generations ago old communion set—and a black choir robe from a disintegrating box, throw it over my shoulder and took the quick walk back to my closet. Back to utility.

The Beloved Community, that's what Allen Dwight Callahan calls it. I found his book, *A Love Supreme*, in the mailroom—an advanced copy, obviously unread. Quite a find. More than I would have expected. It is all about the community of John and the writings that came out of it. A little too perfect, actually. I suspect it is a plant. I looked it over again before I started drilling the holes in the closet door. I am suspicious. I want the stuff that Callahan says to be true. "Across time and space, the writers of that community share vocabulary, stylistic features, and the preoccupation with an idiosyncratic notion of love that they called agape—the greatest of all loves. The community defined this love as putting one's life at the disposal of those one loves. Indeed the community came into being in the love of its founder and early leaders, and in the love of its members for one another: it was a beloved community." Indeed, *indeed.*

The preoccupation with an idiosyncratic notion of love.

Everything is working, so clearly. Not big clarity, but work-of-my-hands clarity. I knew what to do next. I am doing everything at once. I measure out the spot for the hasp, mark where to drill the holes with a pencil, turn to the shelves and see, paint and brushes, perfect. I opened a can of white paint and painted a four-by-six rectangle on the wall opposite the door. When it drys I can use the other paints and the small brushes to get the relevant clues out of my head and up on the wall where I can see them without their moving. *Everything I need, he gives it to me-e-e.* All right here in my utility bunker. Storage. Maintenance. Utility. I find a phone number taped to the fax machine, dial it and heard the guttural trills working their way up to the high pitched *beeeeeeyeeeeeeeeeee* of a fax machine on the line. I want Idiot John's voice, but am forced to write. I write, "I am suspicious of what makes a Beloved Community, beloved. *The preoccupation with an idiosyncratic notion of love.* It almost seems like a way out. —Rev. Lamblove"

I send it off and grab up the drill. The cord is very

short and is stretched taut from the wall socket to the door. I am testing the strength of the electrical tape. I pull the trigger and lean into the drill. It is barely making a dent. I give myself to it, knowing it will be a while before it will penetrate the outside steel and longer even before I can get deep enough in the core for the bolts.

Raymond Brown, biblical scholar and old-time John scholar, makes up a story about the history of the Beloved Community in a book I stole from my Senior Pastor's office. Brown says that the disciple John, called the "one whom Jesus loved" and the "beloved disciple" in John's Gospel, led a group of followers in Jerusalem after Jesus's death and resurrection that was so committed to this *idiosyncratic notion of love* and the restatement of the Law and the Prophets Jesus made, that they were kicked out of the synagogues.

Little curlicues of metal spiral off the bit; I am getting closer. This is the phase that the Gospel of John was written in. Exile from the faith they had held all their lives strengthens their commitment to pursue the new commandment to love the Lord their God with all their heart and to love their neighbor as their self. John moved his beloved community from Jerusalem to Ephesus and likely died shortly after. This was the period, Brown said, during which the First and Second Epistles of John were written. Damn. I am just about to get deep enough and the cord pulls out of the wall. I am, like, a quarter of an inch away and the cord keeps pulling out. I need an extension cord. I am hesitant to leave. I know there must one, some patched together cord in the storage, but what time is it? And what about the footprints? I told myself I'd be fine.

When I come back I check the fax machine, but nothing from Idiot John. Cord extended, I finish hole one and lean into two, which goes much faster. More forward thrust on my part? Weaker metal? I line up hole number three and lean in with too much vigor. It skips off the spot, glances off the door and the bit catches my left cheek. Not too much blood. It feels like there is a little flap of skin, but I don't have a mirror to check or a band aid. A steady trickle, a drip. It'll stop. More carefully this time, I start out slow, a little pressure. Then bring the RPMs up all the way and lean in with all my strength.

The metal curlicues are starting to come. Sometime after the death of the beloved disciple, a rift developed in the community, a break of some sort—at least some kind of argument. This is the phase of the community that produced Tres Juanito. The dispute was over some kind of leadership issue or church structure kind of thing. It was, perhaps, that the church at Ephesus under Demetrious wanted to establish permanent leadership and the Elder wanted to maintain the itinerant leadership that the Beloved Disciple had established, thinking that this was more consistent with the ways of the beloved community. The Elder doesn't even want to write letters. He wants to see each member of the community face to face. Something about the *idiosyncratic notion of love* requires face to face. Actual living people in front of actual living people, talking, looking into one another's eyes.

I finish the holes on the door and then the four on the jamb. I grab the hasp set and the bolts. The fax machine rings, then starts gurgling trill, finds the *beee-yee-yee-beeeeeeeeeee* and starts grinding out the page. I pull it off with out looking at it and duct-tape it to the door so I can see it and consider it while I'm bolting on the hasp. I avert my eyes until I am ready. Finally, I look up to see one word.

Midrash.

What? Of course I have heard of midrash before. I kind of know what it is. Midrash is a kind of Jewish biblical literature or bible commentaries or something. But I have no idea what my insane torturous attorney wants me do to with it. Maybe Idiot John is using it as some kind of code or clue or . . . what is wrong with him? I decide to ignore the fax. I have work to do and I want to stay with the beloved community for a while. I like thinking about the beloved community. They really got it. Though it is hard to believe that the disciples—that band of unschooled ruffians who were clueless the whole time they were *with* the incarnate god—could suddenly absorb this love and transmit it and form a truly beloved community. And where is it now? Why dosen't it persist and transform the world? Why am I in a closet in the sub-basement of this church, the inheritor of said community installing a padlock on the *inside* of the door?

"Indeed the community came into being in the love of its founder and early leaders, and in the love of its members for one another." Indeed-deed-deed.

Alright now, I am ready for anything. I close the hasp, take the lock out of the packing and snap it on. No matter what, I will be able to finish. I put the key in my bag and move on to the next task.

The wall is still a little tacky from the first coat of paint, but just a little. I am ready to start putting some clues on the wall. I have a quart of black, three gallons of blue (a lot of blue), a quart of red, yellow, and a gallon of brown.

In the middle, with the blue—I paint, *the old man*. The old man belongs in the middle. *Follow the victim*, upper left in red. In black along the right side in a column, *phase I—Gospel of John, phase II—Juanitos Uno y Dos, phase III— Tres Juanito*; then a circle around the whole thing in yellow labeled with an arrow pointing toward *the beloved community*. Okay. I turn around, my best runway pivot, looking. Is there anything else, any clues . . . I see the door (padlocked against I don't want to know) with the "Midrash," fax duct taped to it. I continue my revolution to the the shelf with my stolen books. And there, the old one I took from the library, *The Wisdom of the Ancient Rabbis: A Midrash Reader.* A midrash reader? Okay. I don't know what it is all about, but that is a clue it has to go up on the wall. So, just outside the circle on the lower left, in brown—*read the Midrash.*

Studying the words on the wall, cleaning the brushes something becomes clear. Painting words on the wall was ridiculous. I thought it would help. But, how? Help me figure out why this book is in the Bible? I can barley remember caring about it. I feel thick, and I remember feeling this way before. I can't remember when, but it is familiar. A headache grabs me, metallic, The headache is part of the familiar feeling. Also familiar is the need to lie down. The only thing keeping me from collapsing is the aversion my body is registering to the cold, black, mouse-turd-stained cement floor. But even the aversion is losing to the weight pulling me down. *My head hurts.* I splash some water on my face and drink, drink, drink from the faucet.

That was a knock. A knock in the pipes? I turn off the water, listen. Again, no, that is a knocking on the door. The padlock bounces just the littlest bit with each knock. I smile at my forethought and preparation. The smile cracks the dried blood and pulls on the edge of the skin flap. The trickle starts again.

Pacing footsteps, then I can hear the keys in the lock. The handle turns, the door comes open a fraction of an inch, but the padlock holds. I can't help but smile. "I was ahead of you on this one. One, two, three steps ahead," I say, but not out loud. I wipe blood off my check with the flat of my thumb and push it between my teeth, suck on it, and bite it gently. Full two-handed shake on the handle, I can tell.

"I know you're in there. Are you in there? I followed your muddy footprints. When you came home I was happy and when you left right away I got worried. Should I be worried? I am."

A pause. She is pacing, trying to figure out what to do, what tack to take.

"I do have your number; I could call you. I could pick up the fax phone and call you. What is that smell, are you O.K.?"

The smell. That's what is familiar. Paint fumes, the headache, the weight. Now I can smell it. I need ventilation.

"Is this something you need?" She always takes such an understanding approach. I almost want to give up.

"I can wait. If you want I can wait here. I could bring you something. Do you need food? I could bring you food."

A pause.

"Are you O.K., that smell is really strong out here. Is that paint? Are you painting? What are you painting? I hope it's not oil paint, you really need some ventilation."

I really need some ventilation.

"I'll wait a little while."

The space inside the utility closet has changed with her out there. It is other or apart or away. It is smaller and I am smaller and I am darker. I should have gotten more lights, lamps, brighter bulbs. They were on my list. Why didn't I get one thing on my list? Okay, *follow the victim, the old man, phase one, phase two, phase three, read the midrash.*

It is not like I don't know I have a choice. I do have a choice. I could even choose to find this merely interesting—not consuming. I could speak and tell her what I have found and thought. Show her the books and read to her Third John and the Old Man and Second John and tell her about the beloved community. She would like the idea of the beloved community. She is the beloved community. She has a preoccupations with an idiosyncratic *notion of love.* She would put her life at the disposal of the ones she loves. I could write her a note and slip it under the door. Tell her I know she is the beloved community. But writing is the compromise. The Old Man said. But he wrote. Because *it* was supposed to be the compromise. He thought he was compromising. But there was more.

She is up again pacing. She tug on the fax machine cord. "Don't!" I slip and say out loud.

"You're O.K. then? You can hear me? I can believe you are O.K., but this, well, doesn't seem like a very good place to be O.K."

I am not O.K. This was such a good place to be before you came. Now . . .

"I'm, um, I am going to leave. Will you come home?"

Yes.

"Will you come home soon?"

I hope.

A pause.

"Well, I'm leaving now, O.K.?"

No. I'm not O.K.

She pats the door, footsteps fading.

I wait till I am sure that she gone. All the way gone. Out of the parking lot gone. I get the key from my bag, and on my knees, unlock the padlock and push the metal door away from me. I walk on my knees out of the bunker and into the sub-basement antechamber. I sort of roll / fall onto my left side and breath. Close my eyes and breath.

The sun dance was a significant part of the Crow Indian

people's spirituality. It was a spiritual retreat in which a large number of participants would fast, pray and dance for a period of days. They asked for answers to events going on in their lives.

The Dakota believe that the bones of bison they have killed will rise again with new flesh. The soul was seen to reside in the bones of people and animals, and to reduce a living being to a skeleton is equivalent to re-entering the womb of this primordial life—a mystical rebirth.

During the dance the buffalo also has a great role in the visions. The buffalo may knock down a dancer, or the dancer may challenge the buffalo by charging at it. Passing out for too long means one was too afraid to face the buffalo. One must show courage and stand up to the buffalo before the buffalo finds him worthy to give him what he desires. At a certain point the Crow will notice he is seeing through the buffalo's eyes, that he has become one with the buffalo.

When I wake up I am still holding the lock. I still have a headache, but it feels like some time has past. I don't know how much—hours or minutes. I don't have my watch. I don't want to move. So I'll sleep a little more.

Chapter 6

I wake up without opening my eyes. I feel the murderous slab underneath my body cutting into my spine and shoulder blades. I rock my head back and forth slightly. The concrete floor has created a barely perceptible flat spot on the back of my skull. My hands lay on the bare skin of my stomach where my t-shirt has pulled up; my elbows have been driving into the ground all night, or for however long I have slept. There is nothing left of them but crushed cartilage and bone spurs.

I am just starting to surface and I feel something on my face, like on my nose and eyebrows. I open my eyes. A blurry cloud? A piece of paper over my face. It is duct taped to my forehead. I pull it off with one quick band-aid pull and hold it above me at arms length. *Midrash*, it says. Idiot John's fax. This is my duct taping. I mean the fax and the duct. I did duct tape it to the inside of the door, but I don't recall taping it to my forehead. It is possible that I duct taped a piece of paper to my forehead in my sleep. I'll allow it mostly because I don't like the other possibilities.

I hear one of those other possibilities moving around in my bunker. I feel around for the lock on the floor. Damn, it's there. All my careful planning still left me vulnerable to paint fumes. I can see that the door is standing open still, but can't really see in without lifting my head or sitting up. My whole body has a hangover, my head still smoky and metallic.

"Reverend, it's time to get up."

"Idiot John?"

"I am here to help."

I start to sit up, my body bites me, I wince and prop myself up on my elbows. "By duct taping a piece of paper to my head?"

"Yes, I know. Crude but effective."

"Effective for what?"

"Focus, Reverend, you need to focus."

"Focus?" I do need to focus, but I don't know what to focus on. My attorney comes closer and my eyes reclose. I sense him kneel down beside me. And for some reason he speaks in an Irish brogue, "You've got to *read*, reverend. You've got to learn to *read*, man." That's not an Irish brogue. That is Scotty from the U.S.S. Enterprise. Am I making him sound that way? Am I accenting his speech? Is Idiot John actually here talking to me, or am I . . . "Focus on this, fo-cus-on-this."

I open my eyes. He is here, shaking the fax in front of my face. "You have to read."

"Read?" I say.

"Yes. Read. The Midrash. That will teach you, tell you."

He is a very big man, lumbersome, but graceful.

"Midrash," I say, "I know, okay I got it, focus on Midrash, so I can read. Will you help me up?" He grabs my upper arm, crushing the paper around it, and pulls me up with him.

He holds the paper to his chest with one hand and smooths it out with the other. Then hands it back to me.

"You need to eat something. Come on." I follow him into the bunker.

Idiot John has ripped open a brown paper bag and laid it on the workbench. There are four deli sandwiches—two roast beef and two turkey on hard rolls. I can see lettuce and red onion hanging out the sides. Chips, yes there are chips, two dills, a bottle of red wine and two wine glasses.

"Where did you get the glasses?"

"I travel with them."

I sit down on the stool and he leans against the bench.

"The sandwiches are from Cecil's, the wine from my own cellar." He takes a corkscrew out of the inside pocket of his jacket and opens the wine. I reach out to pick up my glass and he puts his hand over it. "Not yet Reverend, you need to hydrate." He produces a bottle of water and hands it to me. "Now tell me about the Juanitos."

"Wait a minute. Tell me about some things first."

"O.K., Midrash . . ."

"Not Midrash, wait on the Midrash. First, *why* are you doing this to me, did you drug me, and who is that Batman guy? How about start there?"

"Batman guy? How long were you down with these paint fumes? As your attorney I advise you to forget the hydration and start drinking now. And I really think you need to reexamine your projection of this adventure on me. I believe my last words to you were more of a warning along the lines of, 'You're not going to start reading the Bible are you?' I think that is what I said."

"What, no, you said . . . you feed me all this stuff about the Juanitos and the anti-Christ, and said, 'Tell me, Reverend, why is this book in the Bible,' and now look at me. I'm messed up. I am really messed up," I say as I finish my wine.

"Try the roast beef," he says. "It has a real creamy horseradish, hot too."

I take a bite of the roast beef. He refills my wine glass, "Ok, yeah, it is really good. That is really a good sandwich. Now tell me what this is about."

"You are asking me what this is all about? I just talked conversationally about an interesting conundrum in the holy writ. It was you who, well . . ."—he looks around the bunker—". . . you who became interested in exploring the matter further. I will just say that I encourage the project and can think of no one else who is better suited for it."

My attorney puts down what is left of his sandwich, stands up and steps over to the wall to examine what I have written. "Alright, this, Reverend, is . . . let me see, *the old man?*"

"The elder from Third John."

"*The old man*. I like it, heart of the matter you figure? Good, I think there is a loose thread to be teased out there. Mm . . . uh the *beloved community*, yes, good. *Follow the victim?*"

"Batman, er, the black friar. He told me that. Follow the victim."

"Who is the victim?"

"I don't know. I haven't thought much about it."

"Well, sit back down and let's get to our business. Oh, there is a thermos of coffee on the workbench right next to the picture of that little girl on the merry-go-round. A niece?"

"No. I stole it."

"What do you mean you stole it? You stole a picture of a scared little girl on a merry-go-round? From where? And why?"

"From the office of one of the other pastors, but I don't know why. Why do you steal anything?"

"I don't steal anything."

"You don't ever just see a thing and think, or not think. Just, like, take it?"

"Um, no. I don't."

"Oh. Well, I just saw it and, you know, took it."

"Why?"

"I don't know. Look at her. She's scared, the way she's holding onto the pole of the carousel horse with both hands. The way her head is turned so she can keep looking at whoever is taking the picture, wanting to stay with them, or wanting them to stay with her, but the merry-go-round keeps going around and she . . . Well, yes, she is scared but it doesn't look like she wants to get off. Is this really the most important thing we could be talking about right now? It's a little down the list for me."

"O.K., top of the list?"

"Actually, thanks for the sandwich. A sandwich can really, sometimes, make everything a whole lot better."

"You are welcome. That is true. Top of the list?"

"I don't know. Like, is it worth pursuing?"

"What?"

"The Juanitos."

"The Juanitos? Chase what you want or what you will, learning to read is about learning to ask questions you don't already know the answers to. But more than that, learning to read is about asking questions you don't know you're asking, about things you don't understand."

"Alright, whatever. What do you want to tell me."? I bring my wine glass to my lips and sip. I take another bite.

"The Students of Rabbi Akiva. Can I tell you?"

"Yes," It's hitting me—the wine and roast beef. "Tell me."

My attorney—smiling as he figures out the last number in the combination—says, "Some time after St. Paul had begun his second missionary journey through Asia minor; after St. Thomas had struck out for India and St. John left Jerusalem taking his, as you say, beloved community to Ephesus. Some time after these things a parallel movement was occurring.

"Rabbi Akiva, who is called by the Talmud, *Rosh la-Chachomim* (Head of all the sages), the father of the Mishna, left Jerusalem, taking with him the twenty-four thousand students in his school. Most of the central leaders of the fledgling Christian church had by this time left the city, which was in the midst of the second great Jewish Revolution. Rabbi Akiva had organized the rebellion after encouraging Bar Kochba, a zealot and big-chested, bearded instigator and motivator of the people. Rabbi Akiva, knew the history and could read. He knew what should and could happen and Bar Kochba would listen to him and, though not following everything he said or waiting for him to finish, would punch his fist into the air and immediately have a battalion at his side. So Rabbi Akiva said to him, and he roared and without much more complications the revolution against Rome began.

But, the rabbi was more interested in the reading and Bar Kochba more into the revolting, so tensions arose. When he wanted to join armies with the Samaritans, Rabbi Akiva could no longer follow, or pursue, or support that which he had instigated. To even consider joining with the Samaritans—ungodly infidels—this, to Rabbi Akvia, was testament that Bar Kochba had abandoned his faith in God for a faith in a movement, a political entity, and politics or an institution. So he took his students and reestablished his school outside of Jerusalem.

"At this point the rabbi was already a very old man. He would live to be 120 years old, the same age as Moses. There are a number of parallels between the great Rabbi and Moses; they were both, for instance, shepherds tending their flocks when they received the call. There are even some intriguing parallels between Rabbi Akiva's life and teachings and that of our Lord

Jesus Christ—Damn! Excuse me."

Idiot John had been gesturing with his sandwich as he talked and in the process loosened a piece of horse-radish covered roast beef, which landed in my wine. He is now fishing it out with his fingers. That done, he ate it, licked his fingers, and leaned forward. "Let's see, the students of Rabbi Akiva. Yes, at this point he was already an old man when he left Jerusalem. The students of Rabbi Akiva were among the greatest scholars of Torah, having studied with the great sage, gaining insights from his wisdom and his methods.

"Some time after the move from the holy city his students began dying of some sort of plague. At first it was just two and then two more and then eight in one day and then twenty-four and then two hundred and forty, eventually all but four of the twenty-four thousand students of Rabbi Akiva died." Idiot John let it hang in the air like he was telling a ghost story.

"It wasn't a plague," I say. "Only his students died and no one else. Why did these great and righteous men, these unparalleled interpreters of Torah die?"

Yes, that is what I asked, but with less drama.

"The Midrash asks the very same question."

"The Midrash?"

"Yes, the Midrash."

"Oh. I should focus on that."

"Well, you should begin to consider it."

"Okay, I will. What is it?"

"What?

"The Midrash."

"The Midrash is both a collection of biblical interpretation and a method of biblical interpretation. It is a way of reading the holy book and a collection of those readings. I am accomplished in many areas but not in Jewish religious literature or Rabbinical Biblical interpretations. I have read deeply, but do not bring the personal history or culture to my study. I am on the outside of what needs to be entered into fully."

"How am I supposed to enter it fully? I've just heard about it. I don't have any, you know, cultural history and deep seated readings and I surely don't have any collections of rabbinical hoo-ha . . ."

"Except this hoo-ha here." Idiot John said pulling *The Wisdom of the Ancient Rabbi's: A Midrash Reader* forward on the shelf out from the other books with his index finger.

"Well, don't you just think of everything."

"I make it a point to be thorough, Reverend."

"So, I should read this book and it will help me . . . how? I don't think the ancient rabbis probably have much to say about the most insignificant book in the *New Testament*. And what makes you think I can enter into it fully if you can't?"

"I think you have the right, um . . . *mentality*. I

99

recognize something in you that might give you a predisposition to their methods."

"Debilitating anxiety?"

I.J. continued, ignoring my comment. "The rabbis, when they read, walk into the text. They bring themselves to it and step across the edge of the scroll onto its body, bouncing a little, believing it will hold their weight. And then on hands and knees crawl through the furrows of words, examining, brushing away dirt, not unlike a botanist examining growth patterns and evidence of the soil's mineral content, water content and whether there is deep clay below the cracks in the soil from which the words emerged. It is the cracks, the gaps, that allows them a way in. The Midrash is the exploration of those gaps. Stories and parables, proverbs and legal case studies come from mining these gaps. The text is changed by their having been there, There are footprints left behind, indentations, great hollowed out places and covered over, smoothed out portions. The tents of opposing camps are set in the text side by side. Conclusions leaned up against refutations, some decaying, some flourishing. Having once been an oral wisdom that required a speaker—and what is an individual speaker if not a unique interpreter—the text was not allowed to pass into stone, to become hardened, but was kept alive and fertile, even malleable. But with deep and unknown roots."

My head hurt. "What the hell are you talking about? Did you memorize that? Or do you just love your metaphorical meanderings?

"Listen, Reverend. That is not how I was taught to read our holy book. I was taught to search for answers—the calculable, defendable, uncontradictable truth, But to the rabbis it is not a book of answers—it is a book of brilliant questions."

"No answers just questions? The rabbis just ask questions?"

"The ancient rabbis read the text as questions and then answer the questions with more questions and provide answers with stories of possibilities. All interpretations are partly wrong and partly right, which is why so many need to be included so that something like truth can be glimpsed or gotten close to.

"Why is it, Reverend, that the students of Rabbi Akiva died? The Midrash says Rabbi Akiva addressed his remaining students and said, 'My sons, the others died because they begrudged one another. Be diligent not to do as they did.' In another Midrash, and this might sound familiar to you, 'Love your fellow as yourself, that is the main principle of the Torah, the rest is commentary.'

"When the Talmud talks about the Rabbi's students it doesn't say there were twenty-four thousand, it says there were twelve thousand pairs of students, because the text is best studied with someone else, with a partner, someone to fight with. So through debate and challenge, disagreement, argument and wrestling the questions can be refined.

"The Talmud interprets the phrase, 'enemies in the gate' from Psalm 127:5 as a reference to people studying Torah together. The gate is the reading table where two students stand next to each other and study the scrolls. 'Even a father and son or a teacher and his student, studying Torah together in one gate become enemies of one another, but they do not move from there until they become devoted friends.'"

"Wait, twenty-four thousand students died because they begrudged each other? What is that? God is punishing begrudging?"

"It's a story and you're missing the point."

"That sounded a little begrudging, I would watch that, counselor."

"First of all, it is clear that you do not know the meaning of the word 'begrudge,' which is to resent, feel aggrieved about, feel bitter about, be annoyed about, be resentful of, grudge, mind, object to, take exception to, regret."

"Begrudge? You want to talk about *begrudging*? Listen to this—and I *like* this guy . . ."

"What guy?"

"The Elder, the Old Man." I took the Bible off the

workbench with my left hand, grabbing at the top, held it up, one-handing it Jimmy-Swaggart-style, reading from the beginning of Dos Juanito.

"'The elder to the elect lady and her children who I love . . .'"

"The elect lady?"

"Yeah."

"Who's she? I kind of forgot about the elect lady."

"This is not the begrudging part, I am getting to it. Forget about the elect lady. I am just starting at the beginning for context."

"But, Reverend, you seem to be ignoring what you are reading for context."

"Okay, but I think you are just trying throw me off my 'begrudging' point."

"No, no, make your *begrudging* point. But you must admit, *the Elect Lady*, that is a mysterious woman entering the story if I ever saw one."

"The Elect Lady is . . . you know probably like, some lady who . . . well if you let me read the whole thing it says, and you'll get the begrudging."

"You really like saying begrudging."

"Listen, O.K.?"

"Old Kinderhook."

"What?" Paint fumes, wine, not enough sleep, Idiot John purposely being an ass. I'm having trouble staying focused.

"Martin Van Buren's nickname was Old Kinder-hook"

"Marin Van Buren?"

"The eighth president of the United States He married his cousin."

"What does that have to do with anything?"

"Nothing, it is just interesting. Can you imagine someone who married his cousin getting elected to-day?"

"Not the cousin thing. Old Kinderhook being Martin Van Buren's nickname."

"Oh, you said O.K.. During the 1840 election his supporters started Old Kinderhook clubs throughout the country to champion his cause, and they became know by their abbreviation O.K., which is the deriva-tion of the colloquialism you used."

This is the kind of information my attorney comes up with all the time. Sometimes it is interesting, but usually it seems to be some kind of tactic. But I never understand the reasons for his tact-ing.

Looking really amused, both by himself and by my consternation, he said, "So since learning this bit of trivia I committed myself to bringing the full nick-name into common usage."

"Yeah, and how is that going?"

"Old Kinderhook."

"The Old Man writes this letter, Dos Juanito . . ."

"You like saying *Juanito* too."

". . . addressed to the Elect Lady, praising her for walking, along with her children, in the truth.

"The truth?"

"I think he means believing the right thing, being on his side of the argument, as opposed to Diotrophes' side of the argument."

"What is the argument?

"Well, it is not completely clear, but it seems like the argument has something to do with Jesus Christ coming in the flesh."

"And the Old Man is for it?"

"It appears so, yes, but here is the begrudging. After praising the Elect Lady for the way she walks he asks her not to let any of his adversaries stay at her house. He prefaces the request with the love commandment . . ."

"Love God and love one another?"

"Yeah, very John."

"I like that."

"The Old Man writes, 'But know, dear lady, I ask you not as though I were writing you a new commandment, but one we have had from the beginning, let us love one another,' you know, this is the commandment you are walking in and should walk in, and in this spirit I ask you to do this thing for me. Then he launches in: 'Many deceivers have gone out into the world . . .'"

"Meaning they left the Old Man and his church or way of thinking?"

"Right. And here is your part, the bait you used to set this hook in my mouth. 'Those who do not confess that Jesus Christ has come in the flesh; any such person is the deceiver and the anti-Christ!' I can see the vein bulge in the Old Man's head. I bet there are spittle stains on the original manuscript. 'Be on guard, so you do not lose what we have worked for, but may receive a full reward.' Like, watch who you hang out with or you get included with the anti-Christers. He continues with the harshities, 'Everyone who does not abide in the teaching of Christ, but goes beyond it, does not have God.' Then he lays down the law, 'Do not receive into the house of welcome anyone who comes to you and does not bring this teaching; for to welcome is to participate in the evil deeds of such a person.'

"And the begrudging point?"

"He is saying, walk in the commandment. The commandment is the new/old one: Love one another. Then he says that anyone who doesn't agree with me is the anti-christ. That doesn't sound very loving-one-another-ish. It sounds begrudging. And if you, dear Elect Lady, have anything do with anyone I designate as the anti-christ, then you will *not have God*. I will begrudge you your choice to love one another."

Idiot John put his chin on his chest, spreading the flesh, looking to be in serious thought then brushing a small sliver of red onion from his shirt. "Yes, very begrudging I agree. Unless the issue is so serious as to require such drastic judgments."

"But so serious as to ignore the 'love one another' commandment? Like it only applies to people who agree with you?"

"Yes, but consider if the error of the Old Man's opponents, Diotrophes as you say, is so great that it must be corrected or it will endanger those who follow it."

I am walking around in small circles. I turn to I.J. with the certainty of proving my point. "Then say, love them, love Diotrophes even though he is wrong, doesn't love conquer all? Don't call him the anti-christ."

"I don't think that is actually in the Bible."

"It is right here, you showed it to me, 'any such person is a deceiver and an anti-christ.'"

"No, the love conquering all part."

I stopped moving, looked at him and rolled my eyes in disgust, then stared at nothing over his left shoulder.

"Yes, you have a point. It is a bit contradictory, harsh, *begrudging*."

"What would Rabbi Akiva say about that?"

"I don't think he would like it."

"Why doesn't God kill the Old Man and his followers?"

"I don't think, as I said earlier, that the point of the story is God killing the twenty-four thousand students of Rabbi Akiva. It is a Midrashic story to illustrate a point about how one should study the text. That disagreements, even vehement disagreements, are necessary to glimpsing the meaning, but in the end love overrules any animosity that comes about in the process."

"Well, you didn't say it quite that clearly earlier, but you are making my point for me. The Old Man disagrees with Diotrophes and his folks, so he is begrudging him. Not arguing like enemies at the gate. The Old Man is begrudging. Worse than begrudging. He is trying to form an alliance with the Elect Lady and her children, whoever they are, and Gauis and whoever is with him, by saying the Diotrophes is the anti-christ. They are trying to make him the scapegoat. 'Look at him. He doesn't have God with him, and we do. He is the anti-christ. We are right and good and walk in love.'

"The Old Man is sacrificing any love he might have had for his enemy at the gate, his Torah study partner, sacrificing Diotrophes, to solidify his place in the *supposed* beloved community."

My attorney raises his hands in front of him, palms up. It's a what-can-I-say, you-have-a-point gesture, but then he turns the palms in and rubs his belly with them. "So, my original questions remains. If what you say is true, why, dear Reverend, is that in the Bible?" He stands up and puts a hand on my shoulder. "If you finish your wine, I'd like to take the glasses with me."

I drain my glass. He holds it upside down by the stem and shakes it, leaving red droplets on my T-shirt and the floor.

"You really have gotten your self into a mess here," he says. I see the grin on his face growing as he turns away from me. Over his shoulder, "Don't forget to lock the door behind me."

Midrash, enemies at the gate. Read the text like a Rabbi.

Chapter 7

Aruite... Dos Juanito... The Elect Lady... Add It
Up... Add It Up... A Bad Puncture Wound... "It's
Just In There."..

I have read *The Wisdom of the Ancient Rabbis*, the
midrash reader . . . and I kind of get it, but . . . well,
there is freedom and there is confusion and I think I
have to read more to understand what part is freedom
and, whether the confusion is the freedom, and also
why it makes me feel zingy.

My therapist's warning about reading the Bible
should apply doubly to reading ancient rabbis reading the Bible, because it makes my head and lower
abdomen move around. It is like my attorney got to
the rabbis with his gun and his pills and the pale ale.
This, an example:

My Readers Gift Bible translation of Exodus 12:3
says, "Tell the whole community of Israel that on the
tenth day of this month each man is to take a lamb
for his family, one for each household." Ok, let's dis-
cuss. "How do you read," is the proper rabbi question.
The starting place, not where I would have guessed,
is: The midrash attaches verse six to verse three, (You

shall keep watch over it until the fourteen day of this month), and then asks, "Why did Scripture require that the lamb be taken four days before it was to be slaughtered?" Like I said . . . But anyway, it kind of goes along and one rabbi says, "It is because the people had no mitzvoth with which to occupy themselves in order to make them worthy of redemption." A mitzvoth, I read from the notes, is any of the 613 laws contained in the Torah. See, they had no law to obey to prove that they could obey a law, thus making themselves worthy of the Passover, the redemption they were about to receive. But then right after that, the next paragraph, Rabbi Eleazar ha-kappar says something like, "Had not Israel already fulfilled four mitzvoth which are of greater worth than the world itself? They were not suspected of sexual misconduct nor of speaking evil, neither had they changed their names or their language." This is what I love., Which of those points would you address? Well, the rabbis would too. They go down into the furrows.

First question: "How do we know that they were not suspect of sexual misconduct?" One possible answer: "As it is said, there came out among the Israelites one whose mother was Israelite and whose father was Egyptian (Leviticus 24:10). This informs us that Israel was praiseworthy in that this was the only case of sexual misconduct among them. That is why Scripture singles it out." My attorney was right, this is the kind of reasoning I can understand—the fact that sexual misconduct is specifically mentioned is the proof that there was no sexual misconduct. And the argument goes on, with more poetic possibilities, citing the Song of Solomon, "A garden locked is my own, my bride, a fountain locked, a sealed up spring. A garden locked refers to the males and a fountain locked to the females. Rabbi Nathan says, that a garden locked refers to those married and a fountain locked to those engaged." And then there is just one other little thing added. "Another interpretation is that a garden locked and a fountain locked refer to two types of intercourse."

Read the text like a Rabbi, Idiot John said. I will do my best, counselor.

I put away the midrash reader, regrettably, but there's work to be done. I place the Readers Gift in front of me.

I have to step across the boundaries of the scroll onto its surface. I sit. I have no enemy at the gate. I wait. Look around. I have a solid, fireproof door with a poorly installed padlock. I have a wall with words painted on it, still perfuming semi toxic odors. I have a stool and a half eaten sandwich and a picture of a scared, open-eyed wondering girl on a merry-go-round. And a pickle. And books. I have a lot of books, I have

Bultman and Callahan and Brown. Maybe they can be my enemies. I have the text itself. I have the Old Man.

I open the Readers Gift Bible to the Second Letter of John and put the Bible on the floor, not thinking this is an odd thing to do, but thinking I don't know what else to do. Thinking, this is contrary to what I have been taught to think about what one should do with a Bible. It is to be respected, pages turned gently, not used as a coaster. I stand in front of it and lift my right foot above it, ready to take a step. This is, I realize, a sign of apostasy. On their early missions to Japan, the priests and converts were taken prisoner and forced to choose between renouncing their faith or death. A Bible was placed on the ground in front of them and the order was given: *Aruite*. Walk. Tread on the Bible. And a lot did. Priests and converts both. I would, given the options. But here there is no threat of death, maybe a promise of life or understanding. Overstanding. I put my foot down. I put all my weight on it, lifting up my left leg, bouncing at the knee, balancing with my arms to the sides and my left leg back, a pretending-to-fly kind of position.

It appears to be impenetrable. I bounce again. I put my left foot back on the ground and step off the Bible with my right. The top page sticks to the bottom of my shoe and rips out. Geez. I sit down and gingerly peel it off my shoe. There it is, the entire book of

Second John, all seven short paragraphs, torn out of the bible, with my footprint on it and some unknown tacky substance. I smooth it out on the workbench and start to read.

The Elder to the Elect Lady and her children, whom I love in the truth, and not only I, but also, all who know the truth, because of the truth that abides in us and will be with us forever.

The Elect Lady: She must be some other member of the church at Ephesus who is still trusted by the Old Man, not yet under the sway or suspicion of Diotrophes. She must also be of the second generation, because she seems to have some authority, some people loyal to her. Her children, the Old Man calls them. Callahan says she is one of the five biblical women celebrated by the Order of the Eastern Star. They call her Electa and hold that she was martyred. She wears red and is the symbol of fervency and commitment. Bultmann says she isn't a lady at all but a church. The Old Man is writing to a church, maybe Ephesus, and her children are the faithful there. I like Electa.

The Old Man seems to have complete trust in her. His praise for her seems less put on than his for Gaius. He wishes her grace, mercy and peace from God the Father and from Jesus Christ the father's son. He couldn't bring himself to invoke the Savior's name in Tres because the letter was a ruse, a test to confirm his suspicions that Gaius had sided with Diotrophes. He was being insincere and would not blaspheme God by invoking God's name for the sake of a scheme.

I am overjoyed to find some of your children walking in the truth, just as we have been commanded to by the Father.

I see, if not a gap, an implication. This letter is the follow up to his little fishing trip to Gaius. Demetrius came back with a report that Gaius had indeed turned to the side of the heretic. Gaius wouldn't offer Demetrius hospitality. But Demetrius was given lodging and hospitality by the Elect Lady. She expressed her sympathies with the Old Man to Demetrius, and she told him there were others as well. But not too many others. He writes, "I am overjoyed to find that *some* of your children . . . Not *all*. Not even *most*, but only *some* of her children are walking (walking?) in the truth. While others are presumably sitting around listening to the heretic, to whom the Old Man soon turns his attention, warning her:

Many deceivers have gone out to the world, those who do not confess Jesus Christ has come in the flesh, any such person is the deceiver and the Antichrist!

There it is. The Antichrist. I look up instinctually, wanting Idiot John back.

In his last letter the Old Man called him evil, but here he coins the phrase that will live on in infamy—

the Antichrist. *Everyone who does not abide in the teaching of Christ, but goes beyond it, does not have God.* Diotrophes, goes beyond the teaching of Christ, he doesn't confess that Jesus Christ has come in the flesh. He is an anti-flesh, antichrist.

Then he warns Electa, *Do not receive into the house or welcome anyone who comes to you and does not bring the right teaching; for to welcome is to participate in the evil deeds of such a person.*

I smooth out the torn page and read it again.

So, in his first letter, (I think Raymond Brown got the order wrong. Tres was written first, then Dos) the Old Man calls Diotrophes evil because he is spreading false charges against him and goes even farther—he refuses to welcome the friends into his home and expels anyone from the church who does. Now in his second letter to Electa, *he* is the one telling her not to welcome people, saying if she does, she will be the same as the Antichrist. Where is the love? Where is the beloved community? Where is the grace and mercy of Jesus Christ the Father's son? Come on Old Man. It doesn't add up. Add it up, add it up.

This is the Elder, the beloved disciple of the beloved disciple? Before he went off on the antichrist, he had just written,

Dear lady, I ask you, not as though I were writing you a new commandment, but one we have had from

the beginning, let us love one another. And this love, that we walk according to his commandments; this is the commandment just as you have heard it from the beginning—you must walk in it.

Walk in it. How does he get from there to, *You are no better than the antichrist if you welcome in love someone I don't agree with?*

He closes this letter the same as the first. *Although I have much to write to you, I would rather not use paper and ink; instead I hope to come to you and talk with you face to face.*

"These letters were the compromise, it wasn't supposed to go any further than that." The old man smiles from the other side of the table. The light is not as bright as I remember it..

I am glad to see him again, "Yeah, I know. You told me that before," I say,

"What are you doing here?" he asks.

"I am trying to find out why the hell Tres Juanitos is in the Bible."

"What?"

"Sorry, John, the third letter of John. Why it's in the bible."

"Why are you doing that?"

"It seemed important."

"When?"

"When I started."

"Does it seem important now?"

"No, not really."

"What seems important now?"

"I don't know. I guess I am wondering how to get out of here."

"Get out of where, Asia Minor? This place? This conundrum you have caught me in?"

"That *I* have caught *you* in?"

"Why did you call Diotrophes the antichrist?"

"I didn't."

"You did to. I read it. Here, it is right here, in the letter, you know 'these letters were the compromise.'"

He leans forward to take the torn page from me. "Huh," he says, holding it out a little and moving his head back to focus. "I didn't write this letter."

"Then who did?" I don't believe him.

"Ask her. It's addressed to her." He shoots his thumb over his shoulder, indicating "her" in the room beyond. It's the woman who had served us drinks and looked at us not unfriendly, more accusingly, earlier.

Her? I want to ask her but I can't see her. She was in the room before and she touched his shoulder and she poured us drinks and she refills them now, but I cannot talk to her the way I can talk to the Old Man. She is not solid the way he is. She is a ghost of an answer, not graspable.

I stand up and walk around in a small circle, not

a circle but an oval, there is room for nothing else. I stop, look at the wall. I walk up to it, touch my nose to it and inhale deeply. I step back to read: *The Old Man*, in the center. Up and to the right, *Phase I—Gospel of John*; *Phase II—Ono y Dos Juanitos*; *Phase III—Tres Juanito*. Across on the left, *Follow the Victim*. A thick, paint-dripping circle around all of it with words and an arrow labeling it the *Beloved Community*, with *Midrash* on the bottom outside the circle. I need to add something, but I am not willing to go all the way with the fume headache again. I am going to have to find something else to write with, which means I am going to have to leave my closet, which I do not want to do. I don't know if I can. I am tired and scared. I have to see it through. To go this far and to quit would make this whole . . . what . . . escapade, seem a little bit crazy. Like I had an attack, an episode and then "realized that holing up in a sub-basement utility closet, after stealing things from my colleagues' offices and painting an odd collection of words on the utility closet wall, all in an attempt to find out why the third letter of John was selected for inclusion in the cannon was not exactly *maintaining equilibrium*, so I collected myself and *got my head together* and started working my mental health program again."

The Sun Dance is a ceremony practiced by a number of

Native Americans. Each tribe has its own distinct rituals and methods of performing the dance, but many of the ceremonies have features in common, including dancing, singing, praying, drumming, the experience of visions, fasting, and in some cases piercing of the chest or back. Most notable for early Western observers was the piercing many young men endure as part of the ritual. Frederick Schwatka wrote about a Sioux Sun Dance he witnessed in the late 1800s:

Each one of the young men presented himself to a medicine-man, who took between his thumb and forefinger a fold of the loose skin of the breast—and then ran a very narrow-bladed or sharp knife through the skin—a stronger skewer of bone, about the size of a carpenter's pencil was inserted. This was tied to a long skin rope fastened, at its other extremity, to the top of the sun-pole in the center of the arena. The whole object of the devotee is to break loose from these fetters. To liberate himself he must tear the skewers through the skin, a horrible task that even with the most resolute may require many hours of torture.

I have to see it through, because I don't want that to be the truth—and in truth I don't think it is true. I don't what to live a life of healthy, wellness or to believe it is even possible or desirable. I will just have to will myself up the two flights of stairs and through the halls to the main office where I know they have an entire cupboard full of Sharpies and fatty Magic Markers in a rainbow of flavors. So I will. I volition. I will myself up. I am up and I unlock the door and start to push it open slowly. But there is an invisible fish line connected to my eyelids, which runs down through some sort of eye hook in my shoe and back up to the doorknob. It begins to pull my eyes closed. *Huh*, I think. Just to test the mechanism I close the door and as I do my eyes open to see the gray age-darkened metal door. I try it again just to make sure this mechanism is actually in place. I put my hand on the doorknob, turn it, and slowly push it open. The corresponding fish line pulls through the eyehook in my shoe, up to its attachment to my eyelids and pulls them closed. I pull the door shut, the tension on the line is released and my eyelids open.

"Well," I think, "this is going to make things more difficult." Or, maybe this is going to make things easier. I don't need to see, to actually see. The church is dark. Navigating by sight is an illusion. It ignores what I actually know. I have walked through this church building, its halls and staircases so many times. My muscles and limbs know them. To see the misshapen and shadowy images of the dark is not to see what is truly there. I know what is there and I can see it even if I don't have sight.

I slowly ease the door open and the tug on my eyelids is not even perceptible. Eyes closed, door open, I decide the only way to make it through this is to run.

Eyes closed, but with true sight, I run.

I misjudge the distance to the bottom stair quite badly. They came up quick (perhaps I run a lot faster than I think), lower shin just above the ankle, damaged. Lip bleeding from the biting of it, from the tripping and striking of my chin on what I am estimating is the fourth step up. I reach for the railing and find it easily, pull myself up and run, taking the stairs several at a time, slipping only five times. I know the door is coming up, so I put my non-railing hand out in front of me. Just a little hyperextension of my middle finger when it hits the door.

I know this next part well, eighteen feet to the right, down the hall to the next set of stairs, which will take me up to the ground level. I really get the wheels moving.

It turns out to be more like twelve feet to the end of the hall. Not unconscious, but flat on my back. I hit the cement block wall pretty hard with my head, at what, I am guessing, was a pretty good rate of speed. I can feel an egg rising on my forehead. Not really any blood that I can feel, but tender to the touch. I hop to my feet, grope for the stairs and the railing with both hands while doing a very high-stepping almost-jog-in-place kind of thing. Left foot hits the top of the first stair, I find the railing with the right hand, grip it high and slingshot myself onto the staircase running hard. There is no door at the top so I don't even slow down. I Wylie Coyote up past the top stair and come down with both feet on the mezzanine floor and pick up speed. It is a wide, long space with nothing to stop me from here to the reception office if I keep to the middle. I misjudge the middle and hit a table—wood by the sound of its breaking. I am prone, half on the table top, half on the hall floor, arms stretched out in front of me, cheek sticking to some kind of glossy brochure by the feel of it. Man, the legs just came right out from under that thing. Snapped right off. I pull my arm back to feel my side. I am guessing some cross support broke off with a jagged edge and that is what is currently sticking in my side. It is not in that far. I pull it out and press my shirt against the opening to help the blood coagulate. My chin is raw, from what was probably a two-foot-long slide on the tabletop after the initial impact. I roll off the tabletop, all the way around, back on to my stomach and push myself up. Ten more feet to go and I will run right into the office door. I put on the brakes just in time. My whole body hits the door at the same time, so the impact is absorbed. I find my keys in my pocket, feel the heads for the diamond-shaped one and then aim it at the door where I think the lock must be. Pretty close, I hit the knob. I baby it in with my other hand, unlock the door, push it open, turn around on the other side, and swing it closed. I hear the lock click on the strike plate and my eyes are pulled open. They have the same kind of fishing line set up in this office, it seems.

There is enough streetlight through the windows to find my way, but I am still cautious about more injuries. The pain is starting to catch up with me. I go around behind the counter and open the supply cupboard. I see everything I need. I grab a red and a black and a blue Sharpie and four super-fat markers in the same colors, plus green. And a bag of rubber bands. I don't need the rubber bands, but it is hard to resist a whole bag of rubber bands.

"I don't like it," the Old Man says from behind me. I get up from my squat and turn around. He is sitting at one of the desks with a Bible open in front of him. I am a little annoyed to see him up here.

"What?" impatient from the pain. "What don't you like?"

"This," he says.

"The Juanitos?"

"I don't like these letters being in here." Then, looking up for the first time, "What happened to you?"

"I ran into something—things." I touch my side involuntarily and wince. I pull my shirt up a little to look.

He leans forward. "That's a bad puncture wound. You should do something about that."

"Yeah, I probably should, but I don't have the time."

"Infections, Reverend," he says sounding a little too much like my attorney. I squint at him.

"I don't like this at all. Why would they put these in the book? Can you tell me that? Why?"

"Look, the last thing I want is to try to answer that question coming from you. You know? Like, why are you asking *me*? Have you not been paying attention to everything I've been doing here? And hey, that woman, in your house . . ."

"It's not my house, really. I walk. I don't have a house."

"But the house I saw you in . . ."

"It's her house."

"Electa's?"

"Who?

"You said she was the woman from the letter, and the letter is addressed to her. Isn't she Electa?"

"I just don't like them being in here. I never even knew . . ."

"Forget it," I say, grabbing the markers and Sharpies and rubber bands from the floor and shoving them in various pockets of my trousers.

"You don't have to be angry with me."

I walk back around the counter and put my hand on the doorknob. "I don't have time right now, Old Kinderhook. I gotta run." I pull the door open, my eyelids come down, and I run.

Chapter 8

I make it back to the closet with only a few more
wounds, the worst resulting from the fall halfway
down the first flight of stairs. I felt the back of my
head bounce off at least five of them. I don't know
exactly what they mean by *slight* when it comes to
concussions, but if anything it is *slight*.

I was happy my eyes opened when I shut the
door—I had a worried that they might not. I snap on
the lock and empty my pockets on the workbench. I
set aside the red marker for Electa, picked up the black
one and popped off the lid. I wanted to do something
with *midrash*, to move it inside the circle. I thought a
minute, kneel down and write it at the inside bottom
of the circle, below the Old Man. The marker squeaks
on the paint. It makes me happy. I cap and toss the
black onto the workbench. Oval around the closet a
few times considering. Walk up to the wall, back-step
away, rock forward, rock back, thinking. Midrash, I like
where it sits down there, like something transcendent.

I had just recently learned in a conversation with

my therapist that the way I use the word *transcendent* is wrong. "Transcendent," she told me, in a way that seemed like she thought it might bear on my mental health, "means to go beyond, to rise above." I had always thought of it as *below*. Like some idea or deity that thoroughly passes through ideas or reality, absorbing them and leaving them simultaneously, until it got to the bottom, the foundation, and then persisted below the foundation somewhere unknown—containing and sustaining all, but unknowingly beyond. Maybe that's where the midrash points.

I am ready for her now. Red Sharpie in hand I reach to the upper left of the circle and write her name, *Electa*. And then I write her name, like, a thousand times. *Electa, Electa, Electa, Electa* . . . in red. I write her name over all the other words, *Electa, Electa, Electa. Electa*. . . .I write her name until she comes to me. I'm writing myself into her room. The same room where I first met the Old Man—her house.

She stands there looking at me. "You can sit down," she says.

"Thanks," I say and sit down on a mat at the table.

"You have questions?"

"Yeah, kind of. Yeah, I guess."

She smiles, and brings out the pitcher and pours us both a drink and sits on the ground across the table from me. "Alright," she says, inviting.

"Well, I just wanted to, you know, understand."

"Understand what?"

"Um, well, I kind of don't know anymore what I might want to understand."

"That's alright. You can just sit a while if you like."

"Thanks, that seems nice." It is unusual to sit face to face across a table from someone without saying anything and for that to be okay. Old Kinderhook. For me anyway. I breathe and I look around the room. Nothing really to look at, but I like it. Cool and shadowy outside, dark through the windows, but the crisp electric liquid light of a big moon pours in. I look at her and I smile a shy smile. I feel like a little kid who's found a mom, or a nice aunt or a nice lady at church he wishes was his mom. Not that I don't like my mom or wish I had a different mom, just that I wish that this woman could sometimes be my mom, because of how her just being there, not even saying anything, makes me feel.

"This is where the Old Man was, before, when I saw him?"

"Yes."

I don't speak right away.

"Do you know about this stuff?" I say gesturing to the wall behind me where I had written all my clues. She laughs a little, and I blush. "I mean, you know, before I wrote your name over the top of everything.

The stuff that was there before."

"Yes, some of it."

I don't ask her more right then. I don't care right now about my frantic search for a final answer to Idiot John's question. Right now it doesn't feel important— just kind of interesting.

We sit.

"More?" She says lifting the pitcher.

"Yeah, thanks."

"Are you hungry?"

"Um, not really."

"Would you have a little bread?"

"Sure, that would be nice."

Electa gets up from the ground, brushes herself off and goes to a low shelf at the other end of the room. She takes a loaf of flat bread from under a cloth and brings it back to the table.

She kneels at the table, looks at me, and smiles. She breaks the bread, puts one half down and picks up my refilled glass, offers me the bread and the cup. My hand touches hers as I take it. I shiver, but it's not cold. It's like warm electricity.

"It's just in there." She says. I take a bite of the bread and a crumb falls into my cup. "You could start with that."

"You mean start with *it's just in there?*"

"Yes."

I look around the utility bunker, the word-covered wall, the workbench strewn with open books and Sharpies and half empty this and thats, fax machine, drill, bag of rubber bands and a picture of a scared little girl on a merry-go-round. She looks a little less scared now, somehow. Electa reaches across the table and touches the raised red lump on my forehead and then my chin, my swollen lip. I put down the bread and the cup and get up on my knees, twisting a little. I pull up my shirt so she can see my wound. She gives it a sympathetic frown. "I can clean that." She gets up and goes for something. When I was a kid and skinned my knee or cut myself, it didn't ever really hurt that bad until I saw my mom. Then I would cry. I never fully felt the pain until it was safe to.

Electa comes back carrying a small bowl of water with some herbs in it and a cloth. She walks around the table and I kind of turn and rise up on my knees. "Just sit back," she says. "We'll get this first," and dips a corner of the cloth in the water and dabs my forehead, my chin and touches it to my lip. It stings a little, but it's cool. I can smell the herbs, how everything is fresh. "Anymore?" she asks. I look at my hands and arms, turn them front and back and then feel around my neck and touch the back of my head. "Ahh."

"Is that kind of tender?"

I gingerly pat it a couple of times with the flats of

my fingers, "Yeah, a little."

"Let me see."

I twist my neck and shoulders around so she can see. "Yes, that is a little angry." She dips the cloth in the water and squeezes it out. She holds it to the back of my head with one hand and rests the other on my shoulder. She looks at my face and in my eyes. "Now let's see your side." I rise up on my knees and pull my shirt up. "A little higher." I bring it up with both hands to my chest. She clucks and frowns, wrings out the cloth, rinses it and wrings it out again and starts dabbing at the wound. I grimace and hold in a sound. "It's okay if it hurts," she says. I don't cry, but I wish I could.

"I have to go," she says.

"Okay," I say, barely audible.

"So just start from there."

"From, *it's just in there?*"

"Yes. It's just in the book."

"And then what?"

"Read it."

"Read it."

"Not with desperation, but just because it is in there."

I stand up from my stool, turn around and look at the wall, at her name. And I cried a little.

"I love her," the Old Man said from behind me.

"Me too." I turned around.

"You look better."

"Yeah."

"Can I talk to you now?"

"Sure," I said, turning back to look at the wall.

"When I first read the letters, when I saw you earlier, I didn't like that they were in there. I was looking at Dos and Tres, as you call them, then I read Uno and I just laughed. They are crazy I thought. Beautiful and crazy."

"Who is?"

"They, the beloved. Have you read the first letter?"

"I have read them all, quite a few times. You know that."

"You should read them again."

"They're just in there."

"Right, they're just in there, and I'm walking."

"Where?"

"I don't know. To find somebody to walk with?"

"I'm gonna sleep a little bit."

"Don't do that, Reverend."

"Why not?"

"It's just not advisable after that kind of repeated head trauma."

"I'm tired."

"As your attorney, I advise you not to sleep. Read the text for me. Tell me how you read it."

I look at Idiot John. I rub my face. The old man

is gone. Idiot John. He practically shines his clothes starched, pressed, clean, crisp, and his hair smelling like expensive shampoo. He looks like he'd just taken a shower and gotten dressed after ten hours of deep, uninterrupted sleep. It wasn't fair.

"I'm on my way to work," he said by way of explanation. "Can you do it?"

"What?"

"How do you read the text, Reverend?"

I stand next him at the workbench, clear a space and set the Bible between us. "You have to start here," I open the book to Third John. "Tres Juanito. Follow the victim." My attorney makes an excited sort of sound in his throat and moves closer to me, looking hard at the text in front of us, looking into it, his shoulder and upper arm touching mine. "Follow the victim," he says with some relish, "I never understood until now how you meant that."

"This letter is written in the aftermath of a lynching, a goat barbeque. A public execution. The Old Man was strung up, and sacrificed to the god of community stability. Equilibrium. The Old Man was a destabilizer, a boat rocker. I don't know what he did or what he was said to have done, but whatever it was, it brought in an element that seriously challenged the community—or maybe the community was moving in a direction away from its origins and the Old Man stood up on a rock and started yelling and waving his arms around and screaming, 'You Are Going The Wrong Way!' But most likely, they weren't going anywhere, they weren't walking, they were sitting and hardening, creating the church, building, they were building something out of stone, unmovable. And the Old Man was shouting, "This is not the way it is supposed to be."'

Idiot John puts his hand, fingers splayed, on top of the text and pushes. "You found that in there."

"Not on top."

He pushes harder. "I am starting to feel something. It gets a little softer below the surface, like soft clay or a road. And there is a fire. Torches."

I put my hand on his. "Torches. People hear the Old Man screaming and the beloved folks start elbowing each other in the ribs, pointing to the screamer on the rock. 'He used to be quite sane. Used to be a hell of a guy, I always liked him. But this new bit with the screaming, I don't know.' And the guy next to him says, 'You know, there's some truth in what he's yelling.' 'Well, yeah,' the other guy says, 'but this is the way it is now, and I like it better, everyone does. And you know being of one accord, that sort of thing, should count for something.' And then a couple of other guys get in on it. And people are starting to raise their voices, maybe there is even a little shoving and a couple more beloveds even get up on the rock and start screaming with the Old Man. So a couple of the higher-ups see this getting a little out-of-hand. The elder, their rabbi, who has been regarded with some suspicion of late, sees that it's going too far and they say to each other, 'We have to do something about this.' And they decide to take the Old Man out—take him down. Diotrophes, being the elder's most beloved disciple—although the Old Man had regarded him with some suspicion of late—stands up on a bigger rock and asks for quiet. Pleads with the Old Man, 'Let me just say a few words, address your complaints, come on.' So the Old Man, being sometimes reasonable, shuts up. 'Thank you,' Diotrophes says. And looks the gathered beloved over in a meaningful way, building up weight for what he is about to say, then turns to the Old Man and stretches out his arm, hand slowly closing to form the finger of judgment and says, 'This man, who we all thought we knew so well is determined to take us all to hades. This man is a heretic!'"

"Wait," Idiot John interrupts, "I thought Diotrophes was the heretic."

"Just listen. This is how I read it. So Diotrophes shouts, 'He knows the truth but has fallen in love with lies. And he spreads this infection with his words and if he is not stopped the whole of our beloved community will burn with this evil. We are all threatened as long as he is here.' The beloved mob erupts with shouts and cheers and they rush the Old Man, his erstwhile companions jumping off the rock and joining the mob. They knock him to the ground. They put horns on his head and tie animal skins to his body. They tie his hands and his feet together and they run an iron rod through him lengthwise, set the fire ablaze with their torches and they roast him. Burn him up until his bones are ashes. And the people are one again. They have worked together to save their beloved community through the sacrifice of a victim."

"Or," my attorney says, rubbing the page of the Bible to get the genie to appear, "maybe it could happened in a more subtle manner."

"You don't think dressing the Old Man up like a goat and barbequing him is subtle? Old Kinderhook, he had begun to express his opinion in the meetings of the beloved community about the slow slouch toward the solidification of the movement. The Way was losing its way. He reminded the gathered that they followed the teachings of a walking, moving, gathering, loving destabilizer and they should return to that way. It was at this point that his own disciple Diotrophes, who had long had other ideas about what the church should become, how it could be sustained and become influential, stood up and said, 'Wise teacher, you have always been my guide and I have followed you mile after mile, through town after town, but I must say, that it is my opinion, that it is time to begin to build the structures that will sustain this beloved way.' The Old Man told him, simply, that he was wrong, but many of the gathered beloved community, who had already been discussing these things with Diotrophes in private, rose to protest the Old Man.

"It was decided that night that the Old Man should go on his way to visit the other churches in other towns and that he should communicate with this beloved community only by letter. The Old Man agreed half out of disgust at their refusal to adhere to his teachings and the teachings of his teacher, and half out of the realization that the beloved community was giving him no choice. It was after he left that Diotrophes and his cohorts began to withhold his letters from the beloved community, and began claiming that he was writing falsehoods and abandoning the teachings of the Christ, in fact, opposing the Christ. They began to call him—"

"The Antichrist," Idiot John interjects.

"Exactly."

"But, Reverend, you have lost yourself. It is the Old Man who calls Diotrophes the Antichrist in Dos."

"No, no, no. The Old Man didn't write that letter."

My attorney lifts his hand from the bible and says, "Here I must return to a more traditional form of biblical exegesis, the plain reading. Tres begins, *The elder* to the beloved *Gaius*. Dos begins, *The elder to the elect lady.* They both conclude with, *I have much to write to you, I would rather not use paper and ink; instead I hope to come to you and talk face to face.* It is obviously written by the same person."

"Yes, it is similar," I said, but why would the Old Man write to Electa, he was staying with her in her house?"

"Where does it say that he was staying with her in his house?"

"Uh, that's in the midrash."

"The midrash? The ancient rabbis have written about the most insignificant books of the New Testament?"

"Yes, the midrash. Listen, the Old Man writes Tres under the name of the elder, even though he has been banished from the community, because that's who he is, and was, and always had been. He doesn't acknowledge the defrocking or excommunicating or whatever it was. He was the elder because he was the disciple of the beloved disciple who was the disciple of the Lord."

"Now, it is *Diotrophes* who writes *Dos*, imitating the Old Man, claiming his place as the new elder of the beloved community."

"Wild speculation."

"Yes, it is wild and untamed. Diotrophes, having

scapegoated the Old Man in the community and run him out, now wants to assure his position by attacking the Old Man's last bastion of support. He knows the Old Man is staying with Electa, so he writes and tells her, *You have shown hospitality to the Antichrist, Diotrophes is the one that coins antichrist, and to continue to do so will make you guilty of all of his evil as well.*

"He is doing the same thing the Old Man accuses him of doing in *Tres*. Remember, the Old Man wrote, *I have written something to the church; but Diotrophes, who likes to put himself first, does not acknowledge our authority. So if I come, I will call attention to what he is doing in spreading false chares against us. And not content with those charges, he refuses to welcome the friends, and even prevents those who want to do so and expels them form the church.*

"Diorophes wouldn't let anyone give hospitality to any friend of the heretic (the former elder, aka, the Old Man) under the threat of expulsion, and now in Dos he is making the same threat to Electa."

My attorney stands there, looking at the blood-red writing on the wall and then at the dried blood on my shirt. He looks at the book and turns back the page, "Then who, Reverend, wrote Uno Juanito?"

"This is the beautiful part. The Holy Spirit."

"The Holy Spirit?"

"Well, the Holy Spirit edited it. Or the beloved

community by the grace of the Spirit of God."

"If that is the case, I have to say that the Holy Spirit is not a very good editor. The book is a mess. It starts out using the plural, as if written by the editorial staff, *we declare to you what was from the beginning, what we have heard, what we have seen with our eyes.* It continues on like that until the end of chapter one and then starts using the singular. Content wise, there are some brilliant, even unique, bits and pieces, but it's rife with endless repetition and contradiction."

"That," I say, bouncing a little on the balls of my feet, "Is the beautiful part. It is the obvious setting down next to each other of completely unrelated texts. Like a bunch of different letters were cut up and pasted together."

"My point exactly."

"And that is exactly what happened. Different letters by two different authors from the same beloved community were spliced together."

"After Electa received Dos Juanito from Diotrophes, she told the Old Man to get his things together. They traveled to Ephesus where she met with Diotrophes. She had gathered all the letters sent to him from the Old Man—letters that he had been withholding—and brought together all the letters that he had written. Then she called everyone in the beloved community together at the rock where they had lynched the Old Man. She asked the Old Man and Diotrophes to stand there side by side, face to face, and she held out all the letters, with the exception of two, one from each of them, which would be Dos and Tres." My attorney nods, and I know he's following me. "And she began to rip them into strips. She let the strips fall to the ground and when all the letters were torn, she mixed them together and then asked everyone in the beloved community one by one to pick up a piece and bring it to her. As they did she began to place them on the flat surface of the rock, in the order that she received them. When all the strips had been laid in place she told Gauis to copy this newly constructed letter exactly as it appears and then she herself added the first chapter using the plural form *we*, writing, *We declare to you what we have seen and heard, so that you also may have fellowship with us and truly our fellowship is with the Father and with his Son Jesus Christ. We are writing these things so that our joy may be complete.*"

"And that, counselor, is how I read the text."

"There are many parts that you missed."

"I know. They're for a different reading."

"I have to ask, why do Dos and Tres make it in?"

"They're just in there. You can't read Ono, unless you know how to read Tres y Dos. Comprende?"

Idiot John puts his arm around my shoulders and

nods his head a little, grinning with the left side of his mouth. Looking around at my utility bunker, he turns back to me like he wants something more.

"This is the beloved community?" I ask, though I know Idiot John can't answer this question. "What makes them the beloved community? They were dedicated to the idiosyncratic notion of love? Yes, but that idiosyncratic notion of love didn't, like, come from them. They are the beloved community because they were loved. Not by each other. Do you know how Uno ends?"

Idiot John clears his throat and then speaks the words as if he had written them, "Little children, keep yourselves from idols."

"Yes. That is how she ends it."

"I like how you read the text." He slaps my back and says, "Off to work for me." And he walks out of the closet. I follow him to the stairs, where he gives an over-the-shoulder toodaloo with his right hand, and, I think, tries to stifle a laugh.

I return to the closet, pull the door shut, pick up my bag and sit down on the stool. Clutching my bag against my chest, I feel the dull outline of something hard. I open my bag and take out the gun. I lay it on the workbench and pick up the picture of the little girl. We smile at each other for a minute and I put it in my bag.

In a time, long after his people had been forced from their homes and made to give up their way of life, made to give up their guns and their ponies, to hunt no more, to live like farmers on an arid land, when fighting was no longer possible, Crazy Horse took only a few of his warriors and left the reservation at night. He traveled to the Black Hills and performed one last Sun Dance. The Black Hills were the most sacred place to the Sioux and they had been taken from them through several deceptive treaties, though Crazy Horse had not signed any of them. His signature never appeared on one treaty. He was known as the-one-who-never-touched-a-pen.

He danced through one night and at sunrise he asked the Great Spirit what he should do. He had fought for so long and was still unable to save his people. He was unable to keep the people on the land, so that the young men and young women could grow and hunt buffalo, to know what it is to live like a Sioux, and to die like a Sioux. Instead they were trapped in a land not their own and made to learn the ways of strangers. The Buffalo came to Crazy Horse and showed him that he could live free, that if he did not go back to his people and their reservation, he could live out the rest of his life on this land like a Sioux and die like a Sioux. Crazy Horse pulled back, ripping the bone from his flesh and fell unconscious. When he came to, he told the warriors with him what the buffalo had shown him. And then he said, "It is time to return to our people."...

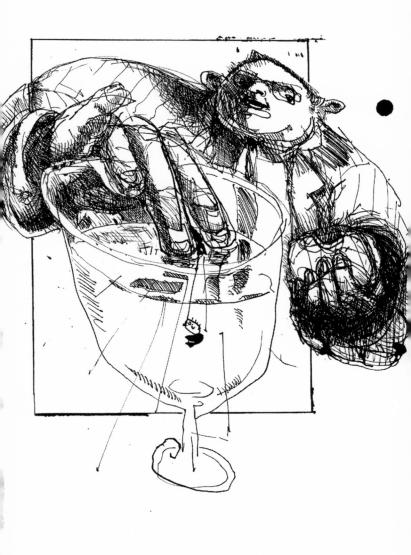

Acknowledgements

This didactic novella would not have been possible with out something to didact. I am especially indebted to the work of English Catholic theologian James Alison, contemporary Torah scholar Avivah Gottlieb Zornberg and Jim Larson, whose drawings add an interpretive layer to this work beyond what I could have conceived and whose paintings read me, always. I was greatly aided in my reading of the *Epistles of John* by, Allen Dwight Callahan's, *A Love Supreme* (Augsburg Fortress, 2005), David Rensberger's, *The Epistles of John* (WJK, 2001), and Rudolf Bultmann's *The Johannine Epistles* (Fortress Press, 1973). as well as countless conversations with my colleague Debbie Blue, who's *From Stone to Living Word* (Brazos Press, 2008) is as good a primer on how to read the text as you'll find. I am grateful to Mike Rathbun, Brett Larson, Jackie DiMeglio, Daniel and Emily Hoisington, all the folks who read the Bible with me at Erin and Jeremy's Tuesday night Bible Study, the patient community of House of Mercy who had to listen to six consecutive sermons on why 3 John has nothing to say, and of course, my attorney.

For Joe, Maria and Jeanne